PRAISE FOR
THE WOLF OF
CAPE FEN

"A stunning seaside fairy tale that will absorb readers until the very end."

—*Booklist*

"A mesmerizing piece of magical realism packed with mystery, suspense, and, most important, love."

—*School Library Journal*

"Debut author Brandt's atmospheric, genre-bending middle-grade novel brings grim fairy-tale magic to a small peninsular town in the early twentieth century."

—*Publishers Weekly*

"This intriguing mystery culminates in a startling, literally transforming climax."

—*Kirkus Reviews*

"Liza's story weaves its magic around you, as wild and wondrous as the dreams at the book's heart. Cape Fen and its inhabitants will haunt you long after the book is closed."

—Cindy Baldwin, author of *Where the Watermelons Grow*

THE WOLF OF CAPE FEN

THE WOLF OF CAPE FEN

JULIANA BRANDT

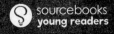

sourcebooks
young readers

Published by Sourcebooks Young Readers, an imprint of Sourcebooks Kids
P.O. Box 4410, Naperville, Illinois 60567-4410
(630) 961-3900
sourcebookskids.com

The Library of Congress has cataloged the hardcover edition as follows:

Names: Brandt, Juliana, author.
Title: Wolf of Cape Fen / Juliana Brandt.
Description: Naperville, Illinois : Sourcebooks Young Readers, [2020] |
    Audience: Ages 8-12. | Audience: Grades 4-6. | Summary: Baron Dire
    haunts Cape Fen, striking magical bargains, demanding unjust payment,
    and sending the Wolf to hunt those who do not pay, but Eliza and Winnie
    Serling are determined to stop him.
Identifiers: LCCN 2019034956
Subjects: CYAC: Magic--Fiction. | Wolves--Fiction. | Fantasy.
Classification: LCC PZ7.1.B75152 Wol 2020 | DDC [Fic]--dc23
LC record available at https://lccn.loc.gov/2019034956

Source of Production: Sheridan Books, Chelsea, Michigan, United States
Date of Production: January 2021
Run Number: 5020426

Printed and bound in the United States of America.
SB 10 9 8 7 6 5 4 3 2 1

To Katie:

You helped shape the world into a place

in which I knew how to live.

And to those who bury deep their dreams:

May you find the strength to dream as loudly as you deserve.

———

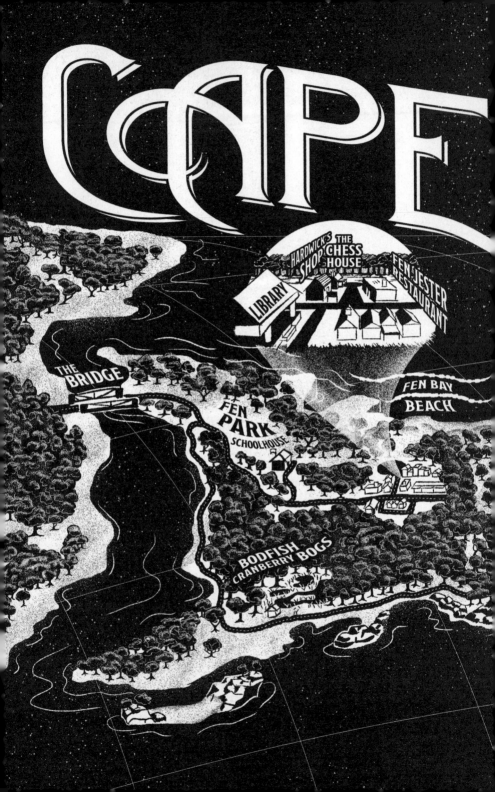

PART I

—

IN WHICH THERE
IS A DEATH

ONE

—

The moon dreamed. Far below it, a ship sailed
toward Cape Fen, magic and moonlight
illuminating a path across the ocean.

The midnight storm laying siege to Cape Fen's shores seemed determined to ruin Eliza Serling's little sister's birthday. Earlier that day the Cape's weather forecaster had watched birds flying inland, racing away from rain clouds that shadowed the ocean. She passed around word that everyone living along the coast should travel to the mainland to wait out the storm. But of course, that was nothing but a cruel joke. No one born on the Cape could leave.

The only fluorescent lamp left on in the Serling home darkened by the force of the storm's winds. The yellow-speckled stars on the stained-glass lampshade dimmed as electricity stuttered inside the Fen Jester Restaurant. It was the only thing of Ma's that had survived Pa's purge after she'd left four years before. Eliza scowled at it now and vowed to use only plain oil lamps in the future. They, at least, didn't stop working when stiff winds blew through their drafty living space in the back of the restaurant.

Eliza climbed out of the makeshift fort she'd built for Winnie and clicked off the lamp, leaving the potbelly stove in their kitchen with its licks of blue and gold flame as their only source of light. Returning to their cotton castle, she sat crisscross behind Winnie and took up the knot she was trying to free from her eight-year-old sister's cloudy hair.

"Have you figured it out yet?" Eliza asked.

"Ostrich?" Win asked.

"No."

"Owl. Octopus. Osprey."

"No. No and no."

Eliza tugged hard at the tight cluster of strands. "I give up. I don't know any other *O* animals."

Eliza grinned. "Opossum."

"Liar! Possum starts with a *P*."

"No, it only sounds like it does. It starts with an *O*."

"You tricked me."

"Does that mean you'd like me to go again, this time without a trick?"

"No, it's my turn." Winnie closed her eyes and felt around on the floor, grabbing up the wooden owl Pa had carved for her birthday. They'd celebrated earlier that night with butter cookies and presents—a Wright brothers tin airplane toy from Eliza and the wooden owl from Pa. She lifted the palm-sized bird in the air and flew it above her head. In the dim glow of the fire, light glimmered against fine details: tiny feathers ran down outstretched wings, massive eyes peered out from a heart-shaped face, and elongated claws clenched over an unseen branch.

Eliza picked at the tricky knot while she waited, guilt slithering through her. When was the last time she'd brushed Win's hair? The tangled mess was Eliza's fault, really. Sometimes, she didn't know what it meant to be an older sister without a mother. For Winnie, she tried to be both, though it made her feel as if she were neither. "I'm thinking of an animal, and it starts with—"

"I'm thinking of an animal," Winnie glared up at her, "and it starts with an *S*."

"Salmon," she guessed. "Starfish. Skunk. Sna—"

Light flared outside their fort, and a half second later, a *boom* sent tremors through the walls of the restaurant. Winnie folded into Eliza, burying the owl against her neck, breathing fast with fear as rain lashed the windows and the roof.

"Snake. Sloth." Eliza rubbed the back of Winnie's head. "Snowy owl. Sea lion. Seal. Sparrow. Spider. Squirrel. Stork. Swan?"

"No, no, no."

"I'm running out of *S* animals here, Win."

"It's something little." Winnie's voice was muffled from where she hid her face against Eliza's knees.

"Little like a mouse?"

"Littler."

"I already said spider. A…stick insect?"

"No."

"I give up. Tell me."

"A centipede!"

Eliza dropped her head into her hands. "Centipede starts with a *C*."

"And possum starts with a *P*."

Eliza laughed. Her sister was too clever for her own good.

Winnie turned back over and eyed the fort's ceiling, as if trying to peer through to the rain outside. "Do you think it's a First Frost storm?"

Old fury ran through Eliza, and she pulled too hard on Winnie's hair, making her sister wince. First Frost arrived at the very start of winter, bringing with it Baron Dire, who was more devil than man, and with him came his strange Wolf. This was why no one in Fen could leave; they supplied the baron with a steady source of magic. In the last century of the Cape's imprisonment, only two people had managed to bargain in the right way to gain freedom from the Cape, one of them being Eliza's mother.

It was Baron Dire who'd made it possible for her to leave, and Eliza hated him for it.

"It doesn't matter if it is First Frost," Eliza said, forcing her hands to loosen their hold on Winnie's hair. "First Frost can come and go. We're safe. We've never bargained. Without one of his bargains in place, Baron Dire and his Wolf can't hurt us. Besides, it sounds like plain old rain outside, no frost or snow included… This snarl is refusing to unknot."

"You could cut it out."

"*No!*" Eliza wouldn't give up as easily as that. "You'd have a bald spot at the back of your head. I'll try using soap to loosen it tomorrow."

Another bolt of lightning sheared through the storm, lighting up the Jester with white heat. Eliza lifted the sheet of their fort just as a second bolt lit the earth, illuminating the edges of the window where the shutters didn't quite reach. Thunder cracked close behind.

She dropped the sheet. "Try to sleep. You need to rest for school tomorrow."

"Do not. I'm noctractal."

"Nocturnal," Eliza corrected. "And no, you aren't. Sleep."

"You're being bossy."

"If I'm not bossy, you won't sleep, and then you'll be grumpy tomorrow."

"Grumpy is better than bossy." Winnie reached for the moon-patterned quilt that covered her feet, drawing it under her chin. "You should sleep and dream too, Liza."

Words stuck inside Eliza, gumming up against her anger at Baron Dire. It had been their Ma's dreams that had taken her from Cape Fen, too, right alongside Dire's magic. She tucked the owl beneath the covers with Winnie and pressed her palm against her sister's forehead. Winnie's fine white hair and pale skin framed her black eyes, the only part of her that resembled Eliza. Neither of them looked much like Pa, and neither of them remembered Ma well enough to know. They had two photographs of her. The first was from when she and Pa had gotten hitched, and the muted black-and-white colors smudged the features of their faces. In the second, Pa stood behind the three Serling girls. Ma sat in the middle, a wide-brimmed hat trimmed in lace positioned carefully atop her head. Eliza stood to her left and Winnie to her right. Everyone smiled.

Eliza didn't do much smiling these days. Not since her own eighth birthday, when Ma nabbed a boat and left their family, deciding that Pa and Winnie and Eliza weren't enough. That her dreams of freedom from Cape Fen and its prisonlike winters mattered more than her family.

"I'm too old for dreams," Eliza whispered, not loud enough for Winnie to hear.

Unlike Ma, Eliza's family mattered more than anything else to her. She needed them, needed Win. Even needed Pa who right now worked through the storm in the tin-roofed shed behind the restaurant. She curled beneath her covers, vowing no matter what turns her life took, she would never bargain for use of Baron Dire's magic and disappear, leaving Winnie all alone.

~

Come morning, heavy, gray clouds stuck to the skeletal oak trees and misted chimney tops lining Old Queen Mae Street. They looked as sleepless as she felt, worn out from the sky's fit of rage the night before.

Winnie walked ahead of Eliza. Her hand-me-down galoshes slipped off and popped back on with each step. *Step-step-HOP.*

She jumped into a deep pool, drenching the hem of her jumper and the wool coat that hung past her knees.

Eliza trailed behind her as they walked to school. The sun would rise soon, not that they'd know it if the clouds refused to pass. This time of the year, when days sucked in their girth and nights billowed out, they left the Fen Jester Restaurant early enough that Winnie could play hide-and-seek in the pools of light cast by newly installed streetlamps. Last night though, the winds had blown a transformer, knocking out power running east on Old Queen Mae Street. The turn of the century saw an update to the town center, but electricity still wasn't as reliable as gas lamps. Because it wasn't, they'd dressed in thick, long-sleeve dresses with rounded Peter Pan collars by the light of a coal-oil lantern. After eating the back-end of a loaf of bread for breakfast, they'd stepped out of the Jester onto a road cloaked in early morning darkness.

Tiredness weighed heavy in Eliza. She'd only managed to trick herself into sleeping after she'd pushed hard at the wound of her mother's leaving, making her angry all over again at Baron Dire and the way he'd left her life a mess.

Eliza dragged her feet down the road.

One, two, three. She counted as she filled up her lungs with air.

Seven, eight, nine. She held her breath.

Eleven, twelve, thirteen. Her pulse slowed. Her thoughts drifted away, and along with them—

"Eliza! I can fly!"

"Winnie?" She broke into a jog, her small sack of school supplies bumping against her spine. Old Queen Mae took a turn, following the curved shape of Fen Bay to the north. Shops closed throughout winter loomed over her, throwing angled shadows across the already dark street. "Winnie? Win!"

"See me, Liza?" Winnie stood atop a three-foot-high stone wall that separated street from woods. With her head tossed back and her arms outstretched, it did indeed appear as if she could fly, if only her bones were hollow and her skin lined with feathers.

Eliza pressed one hand against her chest where her heart beat an unsteady rhythm.

"See me?" Winnie grinned, not knowing that Eliza had nearly died of fear.

"I see you."

One, two, three. She held her breath and counted again to settle.

Winnie leapt off the wall and headed down the path that would take them through the woods and along Fen Bay. Shadows scurried overhead, tree branches crisscrossing to block out what little light existed. The forest was too still, even for the start of winter. There should have been a few chickadees out, at least, or a titmouse or two. Their songs should call the sun to wake. But, except for the crunch of Eliza and Winnie's steps, the world was absent of sound. It was as if they'd stepped into a charcoal drawing, she and Win the only pieces shaded in full color.

They crested a small rise and the trees opened on the north side of the path, and at last, sound reached them. *Whoosh-whoosh-crash!* Winnie climbed on top of a large rock. She stood and held one hand above her brow.

"Come on, Winnie. We need to go. Not much time before school starts," Eliza said.

Winnie rose to her tiptoes and leaned out over the rock.

"Winnie!" Eliza closed the gap between them. "Get down from there."

"I'm looking for pirates." Winnie licked her finger, then held it up to the overcast sky. "Sky pirates in air balloons."

"They'd be in an aeroplane, not a balloon."

"A giant balloon filled with butterflies." Winnie spread her arms above her, as if a balloon floated above her head.

"*Stop.*"

"You're no fun!" Winnie launched from the rock into a muddy puddle and climbed onto a fallen tree.

Eliza rubbed her face. She hadn't had enough sleep to stomach her sister's wild dreamings.

A low growl cut through the quiet, the waves having already faded into background noise.

Winnie squeaked.

Eliza turned, fingers stretching toward Win.

There, to their left at the edge of the tree's opening, stood a monstrous animal.

"Hello, Wolf," Winnie said.

A crown of white tipped its ears and ran down the matted fur across its back. Tufts of grey stuck out from between its claws. It was bigger than the sheep dogs kept at the base of the Cape and bigger than the mini pony one of the summer vacationers liked to keep on a leash.

Winter's First Frost hadn't yet arrived, so how was *the Wolf* standing here?

"Back away, Winnie," Eliza said, low.

The Wolf's snout extended. It snuffled, testing the air. Its yellow eyes tracked her movement as she inched closer to Winnie.

"Hello, you," Winnie said to the beast. She held out her hands, wrists bent and palms up, as if to welcome the Wolf.

Its head cocked at an unearthly angle, just a tad too far.

"We haven't bargained with Baron Dire," Eliza said. "You can't hurt us. You're not allowed. I know the rules."

The Wolf shifted, tail standing on end, ears tilting up and steam spiraling from between finger-length canine teeth.

"*Winnie.*" Eliza's voice trembled.

Winnie grinned and leaned forward, the knot at the back of her head poofing up her hair, looking for all the world as if she were a wild animal herself. The Wolf lowered, head dropping so its shoulder blades jutted into the air.

"Please, don't kill us," Eliza whispered, grasping with both hands for her sister. "*Please.* We haven't bargained."

The Wolf leaped. Flesh and blood and muscle launched at Winnie. Eliza shouldered into her, knocking her off her perch. The Wolf sailed through air. Its jaws came unhinged, baring each fang at Eliza, who now stood where Winnie had been.

"*Look!*" Winnie cried.

Eliza couldn't look, but she felt it all the same: the clouds opened above, dawn light streaming down to save them.

And the Wolf passed straight through Eliza's body.

TWO

—

The Wolf of Cape Fen dreamed. It waded belly-high in
water that glittered with moonlight. The night smelled
of footprints left behind by frightened creatures.
The Wolf sang to the sky. It was time to hunt.

Eliza staggered. She patted her chest, but she was whole, unharmed, and unbelievably, *alive*. She looked behind her. The woods stood empty.

She turned to Winnie, arms outstretched to snatch her up in a suffocating hug.

Winnie backed away, her dark eyes widening. She rubbed

at her head, her cross expression more searing than the Wolf's bared teeth. "You shouldn't've done that," Winnie said. "You shouldn't've pushed me over."

"I had to save you!" Eliza's arms stayed raised. She didn't know what to do with them.

"It wasn't going to hurt us. It went *through* you and then disappeared. It's a ghost wolf."

"Ghost wolves aren't real," Eliza said. But the baron's magical Wolf was, and the Wolf wasn't supposed to arrive until winter's First Frost had hit. Eliza could've sworn the storm last night hadn't been a First Frost storm.

Eliza shoved awkward hands into her coat pockets to pick at an undone seam in the quilted lining of her wool overcoat.

The Wolf can't come out during the day, Cape Fen's lore said. *The sun's rays burn through the night's magic.*

Eliza knew the next part, the part lore didn't include—that in the century-long history of the Wolf's presence on the Cape, it had never attacked on a whim. It was this that scared her more than anything else. If it had launched itself at Winnie, there must be a reason why.

Eliza steeled herself and forced out the question, "Winnie, have you bargained?"

Winnie tensed. "I don't even know *how* to bargain."

Accepting Winnie's answer, Eliza hurried them both to

school, thinking it would've been easier if Winnie had bargained after all. That, at least, would've provided a clear answer for why the Wolf had attacked.

In truth, Eliza didn't know how to bargain either. It wasn't something that either Cape Fen's lore or its gossip ever explained. All Eliza understood was that sometimes, if someone met with Baron Dire and bargained for use of his magic, the Wolf got involved. The *only* reason the Wolf ever attacked was because of Baron Dire.

His magic bargains never came for free.

~

They arrived at the schoolhouse after class had begun, dawn already spreading hazy light over the red cardinals painted in the corners of the shutters. Winnie leapt up the steps and hauled open the door, letting in a burst of cold air. Miss Alayna stood in the front reading from a thick astronomy book, her pregnant belly pushing out the folds of her dress.

Miss Alayna closed the book, one finger crooked over the spine to hold her page. "Did we take our time this morning?"

"We saw the Wolf!" Winnie blurted.

The long braid that held Miss Alayna's blue-black hair away from her face slid over her shoulder as she leaned toward Winnie. Their teacher had stayed past First Frost last year and because of it, was now stuck on Fen along with the rest of them. She would know well enough what it meant that the Wolf had returned. She said, "The Wolf is not something to lie about, Winnie."

"I'm not lying!" Winnie's small fists clenched with fury.

"Making up stories is the same thing as lying."

"She's *not*." Eliza quivered with fury as well, which she tamped down into a well-worn groove inside her belly. "We saw the Wolf on the path in the woods."

Miss Alayna's stiff posture said *angry*, and the harsh lines that etched the smooth skin beside her mouth said *very angry*. "Dreams are best left for the night, Serling girls. Whatever shapes you saw in the woods can stay in the woods. If the Wolf were here, we would know of it. Sheriff Olavi would have called. Now close the door. You're letting out all the warmth."

Eliza obeyed, not liking the dark tone to their teacher's voice. She shut the door and pushed Winnie in front of her, hurrying her past their classmates. Her gaze never left the back of Winnie's head, carefully avoiding eye contact with the boy at the end of the aisle. Miss Alayna watched their progress and, once they'd sat, continued to read as if they hadn't interrupted her lessons.

Eliza sat at her desk and Filemon Hardwick sat behind her, just as he had since they first started attending school.

They'd been friends once, when they were about Winnie's age. Friendship had been easy when they were little—*everything* had been easy when she was little, she'd just been too little to know it.

It had been a long time since Eliza had understood how to be friends with Filemon. Her mother was one of the two Fenians who had managed to escape the island's magical barrier, and Filemon's elder brother was the other. Most people thought they should be best friends because of this, that having a disappeared mother was the same thing as having a disappeared brother. It wasn't though.

"You shouldn't have taken the path through the woods," Filemon whispered behind her. His breath rustled the back of her hair; he must be leaning close.

Eliza slid to the edge of her seat, not liking the bossy manner in which Filemon spoke.

"Should've ridden your bike," he added.

Eliza's fingers curled over the lip of her desk and gripped hard. Her desktop was attached to the chair in front of her, just as Filemon's desk was attached to the back of *her* chair. Each unit was chair with desk at the back, which made for easy maneuvering when Miss Alayna wanted to change the rows of desks in the room.

"Probably shouldn't have bargained with Baron Dire either, if you didn't want the Wolf to attack."

Eliza pushed against her desk. Her chair scooted back, making Filemon's desk ram into his stomach. He gave a small yelp, and though he bit down on it fast, it still drew Miss Alayna's attention. Miss Alayna's eyes narrowed at him, and the whole classroom seemed to freeze. Even when she continued on, Eliza could feel Filemon's tension behind her. After all, it was his elder brother, Bri Hardwick, who'd proposed to Miss Alayna, gotten her pregnant, and then disappeared off the Cape to go to university somewhere on the continent.

By the time the lesson ended and lunch arrived, Eliza's mind was numb from the astronomy she cared little about.

To Winnie, she said, "What does it matter if the moon circles the earth or the sun? None of it changes what happens down here."

"Shh, don't listen to her; she doesn't mean it." Winnie leaned toward the window, speaking directly to the cool winter sun. "I think it's interesting."

Eliza started to pull out their lunch, but before she could unwrap it, Colby Parlett, their older cousin, walked between the rows of desks and squatted in front of Eliza. Colby's father and Eliza's mother were siblings, but the families rarely saw one another. Pa had long since forbidden them from talking with Ma's side of the family. For some reason, the Parletts understood more about Dire's magic and the way his bargains worked than anyone else. If Ma hadn't left, she would be here to help save Winnie, but because she wasn't, Eliza had to do it alone, and she certainly couldn't ask her estranged family for help.

"You saw the Wolf?" Colby asked.

Eliza stared into her cousin's too-glossy eyes. Colby always looked as if she'd been crying or staring into a hard wind.

"We saw it," Winnie said.

Colby cocked her head to the side, reminding Eliza of the Wolf—all animal and strange. "Tell me everything."

"No," Eliza said. She gripped Winnie's arm, Pa's warning in her head.

Colby's watery gaze didn't waver, and she didn't blink, holding still long enough that Eliza got the eerie impression she saw through her to the wall behind.

Eliza looked like Colby, both of them with large bones and dense muscle made to weather the cold of winter, not at all like Winnie who was light as a feather. The dress Colby wore pooled on the floor, the gauzy, gray material at the hem and wrists reminding Eliza of spiderwebs, so much fancier than the plain dress Eliza wore. They should've been the same—both were firstborns and both had to care for their younger siblings. But Colby had freedom where Eliza didn't, and Eliza... She was jealous of the way Colby could leave her siblings on the other side of the room without fear of them being eaten by a wolf.

Except—Eliza's fingers twitched against Winnie's arm—maybe Colby *did* fear that. No one on the Cape knew more about the Wolf or its master than the Parletts, and no one's family was rumored to have bargained more.

Eliza released Winnie's arm, and that was all the permission Winnie needed: the story of the Wolf spilled free. "…and then it sailed straight through Eliza, disappearing with a *poof*. It's a ghost wolf."

"It's not a ghost," Eliza said.

"What else can disappear besides ghosts?"

"Wolves, apparently," Colby said. Then she nodded, as if wolves disappeared midpounce every day, as if the laws of science Miss Alayna taught didn't apply during winter when the devil vacationed on Cape Fen's shores. She blinked, perhaps for the first time, and said, "The Wolf only attacks when someone's bargained with Baron Dire."

"I know that," Eliza said. "*Everyone* knows that."

"And if you didn't bargain, why did it attack?" Colby asked Winnie.

Winnie's mouth opened and stayed that way, as if the question hadn't occurred to her.

"Are you coming over for dinner?" Colby asked, like there was any chance Eliza's father would let them.

"We're invited?" Winnie asked.

"You're always invited," Colby said.

"We're having dinner at home," Eliza said, before Winnie could accept.

"If I were you, I wouldn't accept the offer either." The smallest lopsided smile lifted a corner of Colby's mouth. "If you ever need anything, you know where to find me." She stood and rejoined her sister and brother on the other side of the room, stealing away with Eliza and Winnie's story of the Wolf. Eliza shuddered, glad to be rid of Colby's tear-slickened eyes and the way she reminded Eliza of how little she understood the Parletts.

THREE

*Winnie dreamed. Air flowed beneath her body and
passed over her wings. Strong muscles propelled
her forward, lifting her into the sky. She flew.*

Miss Alayna disappeared into a back room as soon as the
school day ended, telling Eliza she wasn't willing to hear
another word about the Wolf.

Behind her, Filemon stood from his seat and shrugged on
his brother's large work coat, rolling up the duck cloth sleeves
so his hands poked free. Eliza remembered he'd begun wearing

it the day after Bri left the Cape, and even in midsummer, he carried it wherever he went.

"I'd like to come with you," Filemon said, without looking up.

"No," Eliza said.

"Come where?" Winnie asked.

"You're going to go after the Wolf." Filemon glanced up, a smudge of lead marring his temple, right beside a thick curl of brown hair.

Eliza's fingers itched to rub it away, as she would for Winnie, but she fisted her hands and hid them behind her back. She said, "It's not possible to go after the Wolf. It's magic, and besides, it's daytime. Everyone knows the Wolf doesn't come out during day."

"Sure, but you're going to go do *something,* and I want to come along."

"I don't need your help."

"I'm not offering help."

"I can help," Winnie said. "I'm good at helping."

Filemon glanced at Win.

"What am I helping with?" Winnie asked.

"The Wolf," Filemon said.

"*No one's* helping with the Wolf!" Eliza wrenched her book bag from beneath her desk and slung it over one shoulder. "*I'm* going to figure out the Wolf, and no, neither of you are helping."

Filemon grinned. "I knew it. I heard the whole story Winnie

told, and I knew you were going to go try to hunt it down or something else equally silly."

Eliza grabbed Winnie's hand and started to tow her toward the front door. "You shouldn't eavesdrop when people are talking with their cousin."

"You sit in front of me! I couldn't very well avoid hearing your conversation," Filemon said. "Let me come along. You'll hardly notice me."

As if Eliza couldn't *not* notice him. She always noticed him when he was around. Pulling Winnie out the front door, she grinned when she saw Basil Hardwick, Filemon's father, standing out front with his hands pushed deep into the pockets of his black overalls.

Saved, Eliza thought, even as she said, "Good afternoon, Mr. Hardwick."

He gave a curt nod, relaxing visibly when Filemon stepped out the front door.

Filemon's shoulders drooped inside his brother's coat. "Hello, Dad."

"I'll be glad to walk you girls home, along with Filemon," Mr. Hardwick said. He did odd jobs around Cape Fen, but most recently, he'd been trained to maintain the electric transformers that spread electricity around the Cape. But no matter what work he did, he always walked Filemon to and from school.

"That's all right," Eliza said. "We have to run a few errands for our pa. Thank you though."

Filemon turned to her, his back to his dad. His eyes were wider than normal, a bit desperate around the edges. "Think about it, will you? I know you don't much like having help, but the next time you go out, I could come along."

"I don't see the purpose," Eliza said.

"Just think about it. I—"

"*Filemon*," Mr. Hardwick said.

Filemon turned, not saying goodbye to Eliza or Winnie, and joined his father, his gait stiff as they walked down the street.

Filemon had been right: Eliza *was* going off to do something related to the Wolf. She knew of no other way to protect her sister from whatever was going on than to start digging up clues as to why the Wolf had attacked. First, she needed to return to the scene of the crime before evidence disappeared beneath the ground that was still spongy and wet from the storm the night before. Together, she and Winnie headed back down the path to the place they'd first spotted the Wolf. There, she stared at a set of huge prints in the damp earth, embedded there the moment the Wolf jumped. The prints told her nothing except that its feet were larger than her own shoes. It had been real. No ghost could leave tracks like that.

"Pa will be mad we're looking for clues," Winnie said as

she dug her fingers into the wet bark of a tree. "He doesn't like the Wolf."

"No one likes the Wolf, and if Pa's mad, he'll be mad at me, not you." Eliza kept her gaze on the large footprint she'd placed directly between her own two feet. Admitting to the awful truth of being the eldest, she said, "I'm the one in charge, which means responsibility for any and all choices Pa doesn't like will fall on my head."

"What's that?" Winnie asked.

"Responsibility?"

"No, *that*."

Eliza looked up, following the point of Winnie's hand, past the edge of the forest. Far over on the rocky beach, three people stood in a close cluster.

"It's Sheriff Olavi Bilson and the Nyes—" Eliza's sentence snagged somewhere in her throat. Three people stood on the beach, but a fourth *lay* on it.

Grim expectation filled her as her feet led her closer to something she wasn't sure she wanted to see. Her sister followed, leaving behind the woods and wading into the knee-high dune grass that poked free of the rocky beach, not making a peep.

"It's Aunt Loretta's husband, Kendare Lovell," Eliza whispered. She recognized his white jacket. He always wore it when he delivered milk, though he hadn't worn it when he'd proposed to her aunt two years ago at the park. Loretta had said yes, though she hadn't smiled when she'd done so. Neither Eliza nor Winnie knew him well, and Pa hadn't allowed them to attend the wedding.

"Is he sleeping?" Winnie murmured.

"No one sleeps facedown in the rocks." Memories of the Wolf churned through Eliza, turning her stomach nervous and sick. Had the Wolf tracked down Kendare right before trying to track down Winnie?

They drew nearer, and Kendare's motionless form came into focus. Eliza froze and put her arms out to stop Winnie from looking more at Kendare's body. She'd wanted to look for clues about the Wolf, though she hadn't believed that *clues* might mean *death*. This, she couldn't allow Winnie to see.

"Stay," Eliza said. A storm brewed in Winnie's face, but before she could argue, Eliza added, "I'll distract Pa tonight so you can climb up and see the stars. Okay? Just stay."

Winnie tilted her chin down and peered at Eliza from beneath her brow. "You're tricking me."

"I'm not. I'm making you a good deal. Take it. Please."

Win gave a sharp nod, and Eliza turned on shaking legs to head the rest of the way to Kendare before she could change her mind. She'd seen him just days before, swimming through the ocean, stretching toward the mouth of the bay and the point over which Fenians couldn't cross. This summer, Kendare's obsession with the water and the barrier had grown, and he'd swum enough to draw the attention of vacationers.

Eliza stepped close, moving too quietly for the distracted adults to hear. The brass buttons on the cuffs of Kendare's white jacket glinted in the afternoon light and thread ran up the back of his coat and along the collar. Atop his head, his mussed hair fluttered in the wind, revealing the skin of his neck, a pallor that reminded Eliza of ash gathered from a potbelly stove. He wasn't bloated, not like old Mr. Haagerty had been when he drowned last summer. The entire town had come out when the man was pulled from the ocean; Eliza still struggled to forget the horridness. Kendare didn't look as if he'd drowned, which meant the Wolf could be to blame.

The group on the beach finally noticed her. Sheriff Olavi Bilson turned, expression souring as she focused on Eliza. Her silver-streaked hair was drawn into a severe bun that sat low beneath her wide-brimmed sheriff's hat.

"Move away from there!" Sheriff Olavi stalked over and grabbed the back of Eliza's coat, hauling her away from Kendare. "You need to get back to your pa, littling. Shouldn't be out by yourself this time of the year."

"We're safe with the sun out," Eliza said. *And I'm not that little*, she wanted to add. Except she knew if she said that,

Sheriff Olavi would say, *You aren't even past your twelfth birthday.* And that would make Eliza furious. She would be twelve in one week! As if being twelve would change anything.

Sheriff Olavi bent to look Eliza in the face, drawing near enough for Eliza to count the specks of sand sitting just beneath her right eye. "You need to go home."

Eliza's stubbornness increased. To help Winnie, she needed to understand if the Wolf was to blame. Besides, all of Cape Fen would know every single detail of Kendare's death by dinnertime, what with the Nye brothers standing on the beach. They gossiped worse than Mrs. Chess, and Mrs. Chess was the Cape's phone operator *and* wrote the newspaper's gossip column.

"Eliza!" Sheriff Olavi said. "Go home to your pa! Don't you dare stay out here a minute longer. If I have to stop by tonight and tell him you didn't listen to me, he'll lock you in your room for a month."

Pa might be mad, but he would never punish her. If he did lock her away, it'd only make more work for him. He'd have to look after Winnie, do all her chores around the Jester, and sift through the herbs that made up his sleeping draught on his own.

"We saw the Wolf," came Winnie's soft voice from behind her.

Eliza reached for Winnie without looking, startled when

a stick met her grasp instead of a hand. She turned and shook loose the twiggy branch Winnie gripped tight.

"We took the path to school," Winnie said, "and the Wolf was there, and it jumped at us, but then it disappeared, and I really think it was just going to say hello, though Liza thinks it wanted to eat me—"

"Winnifred Serling. *Hush*," Sheriff Olavi said.

"But the Wolf—"

"We know about the Wolf." Sheriff Olavi's posture shifted, turning angry as Miss Alayna had been that morning.

If they knew about the Wolf, why weren't they doing anything?

"You both need to *go*." Sheriff Olavi's eyes shuttered.

Frustrated, Eliza wrapped her pointer finger around Winnie's pinky and pulled her away, heading back up the beach.

"What were you doing with the stick anyway?" she asked, remembering the twiggy branch she'd peeled from her sister's grip.

"I dunno," Winnie said. "Maybe I wanted to see if I could make Kendare get up."

Eliza mashed her lips together to bottle up the scolding that jumped into her mouth. Truly, she wasn't surprised her sister nearly poked the uncle they'd barely known with a stick.

One, two, three. Eliza held her breath as they walked the

path back home, trying to still her thoughts in the same way she could still her lungs.

Sixteen, seventeen, eighteen. She watched Winnie from the corner of her eyes.

Thirty-two, thirty-three, thirty-four. She admitted the terrible truth that wound her tight: if they'd left home ten minutes earlier and had been in the woods longer without the protection of the sun, Winnie might be dead—just like Kendare.

FOUR

—

Sheriff Olavi dreamed. She stepped into Fen Bay,
her feet and legs transforming into the long tail of a
dolphin. In the distance, the Wolf howled, and instead of
drifting into the ocean, she struggled back to the beach.
"If I sleep, I can't hunt," she murmured to the thick,
foggy air that surrounded her. "And if I can't hunt,
I'll never catch the Wolf, and if I can't catch the Wolf,
I'll never keep my town safe." She shook off drops of
water, clasped her rifle between her hands, and tracked
the massive prints of the Wolf through her dream.

B y dinner, Mr. Hardwick had fixed the blown electrical transformer on Old Queen Mae Street. Now, by the yellowing light of a fluorescent bulb, Eliza tried to use soap and a comb to untangle the knot at the back of Winnie's hair.

"See, you'll have to cut it all off like Pa does to his hair in the summer," Winnie said.

"Your ears will get cold without it." Eliza stared at the nest of hair, horrified all over again that she'd failed in such a simple way.

The phone in the Jester rang, distracting Eliza and saving her from having to decide what to do about Winnie's hair. Across the room, Pa pushed his heavy frame away from the bar and ripped the squalling device from the box on the wall.

"*Party line!*" Sheriff Olavi's strong voice came out reedy through the phone.

"I'm here," said Pa.

"Here!" said another voice.

"Here," said a third.

Everyone who lived on Old Queen Mae had wall phones, all connected on the same wire. When a line rang in one home, it rang in all their homes.

Pa held out the phone so Eliza and Winnie could listen as more voices announced their arrival.

Sheriff Olavi said, "First Frost hit last night during the storm."

Eliza wrapped her arms around her waist, hugging herself tight. She'd been wrong about the storm, after all.

"Zilpha Parlett discovered winter's Frost down on the Cape's edge this morning, covering the roofs of the closed-up winter homes. Her motorcar stalled, and with the electricity out and the phone lines not working, she couldn't call—"

"Get to the point, Olavi." Pa's white-knuckled hand gripped the receiver. "We know the baron's Wolf was here."

Silence crackled through the line. Then: "Did Eliza tell you?"

Eliza stepped back as if shoved. She hadn't yet figured out how to tell Pa about the Wolf.

Pa glanced at her and frowned, wrinkles scouring the loose skin of his face. "Don't know why you're dragging my daughter into this conversation, Olavi. The Nyes stopped by here earlier, and if they stopped by here, they probably stopped by everywhere, which means the whole town knows more about Kendare's death than what you're giving us in this conversation. Best tell us what you know."

Sheriff Olavi grumbled but reported what details about Kendare's death she could: he was found on the beach midday by one of the Nye brothers, and though the Wolf had obviously been on the beach—its footprints were everywhere—Doctor Landis didn't believe it was to blame.

"Doctor Landis found no teeth marks or blood on the

body," Sheriff Olavi said. "Nothing to indicate the Wolf's direct involvement."

Eliza and Winnie glanced at each other in surprise just as someone snorted into the line and said, "You know the Wolf doesn't have to kill with teeth or claws. Go ask Mrs. Chess if Kendare Lovell bargained with Dire. She knows all the gossip."

"Don't you worry yourself over that matter. I'm looking into it." Someone else tried to interrupt, but Sheriff Olavi barreled on. "Kendare Lovell's parents are trying to find someone to help with the milk deliveries, so it might be a few days before it runs again. Everyone will have to make do with what they've got. The First Frost gathering will be held at eleven tomorrow. No school for all of Friday then, though Miss Alayna's unhappy about it. Starting Monday, school will start at nine instead of eight for winter hours." She hung up, probably to go call the next street on the Cape.

"What about Aunt Loretta?" Winnie asked.

"I'm sure your Aunt Loretta is fine. Kendare was her second husband, and I'm not sure how much she really liked him," Pa said.

Eliza shifted away from Pa. She knew he didn't like the Parletts, but she thought he'd show at least a little kindness toward Loretta.

Pa settled the phone receiver and asked, "Were you planning on telling me about the Wolf?"

"No," Winnie said.

"*Yes*," Eliza said, miming at Winnie to hush. This conversation would go smoother if they made Pa believe they were planning on telling the truth.

"You didn't think it an important part of your day to share sooner?" he said.

Winnie frowned. "You didn't ask about our day."

"I'm asking now." He sat with a thump at the bar and pushed away his dinner bowl.

And so, not for the first time that day, the Serling girls told the worn tale of the Wolf. When they got to the end, Pa was supporting his chin with his hand, and his gaze was focused tight on Winnie. He said, "The Wolf went for you."

"Only like a hug, like a dog that wants to lick your face," Winnie said.

"It did *not* want to hug you!" Eliza said. "Stop saying it just wanted to say hello."

Winnie glanced away. She fiddled with the knot of hair Eliza didn't know how to fix.

"What are we supposed to do, Pa?" Eliza asked.

"Did you make a bargain with Baron Dire?" Pa asked Winnie.

Win's brows knitted together. "No."

"And you, Eliza?"

Shocked anger poured through Eliza. "What does that matter? You can't bargain away other people. Bargains don't work like that."

Pa examined Eliza, then shifted his watchful gaze back to Winnie. It tugged at her in a wholly uncomfortable way and made her wonder if, indeed, bargains *could* work like that. Could someone bargain away another person's life?

"Pa?" Eliza asked.

"I wouldn't worry, Eliza. Winnie should be safe."

"*Should* be safe?"

Pa shuffled around the bar with his dinner bowl and dropped it into the sink behind the counter. "You must've been mistaken this morning. Maybe the Wolf leapt for another reason. Maybe it was going after a rabbit. Maybe it was running through the woods and passed by quickly, and you were startled. Neither of you should be worried. None of us have bargained."

"It's not true though that none of us bargained," Winnie said. "Ma did."

Eliza's knees buckled, and she thumped down on a stool. Hearing Winnie talk easily about their mother's leaving made Eliza sick. She said quietly, "Ma left four years ago, Winnie. It was a *long* time ago."

Pa came back around the bar and stood in front of his daughters. He opened his mouth, and Eliza tensed. Would this be the moment that for once, Pa would tell the truth about their mother and how she was able to get off the Cape?

He placed one hand on both their shoulders, then said, "I don't want either of you scared about this or trying to find answers to questions that don't exist. Baron Dire doesn't play fair, and I don't want you mixed up in his schemes." A flash of anger crossed his face, then got swallowed behind a smooth mask. He squeezed their shoulders. Patted Winnie on the head. Turned and said, "I best get back to work," before walking out the back door to return to his shed that had once belonged to Ma.

"I guess we won't worry?" Winnie asked as she chewed the inside of one cheek.

"I guess not," Eliza said. Except she had too many questions swirling around in her head to put her worry to rest: Was it possible to trade away someone else's life? Was it possible to bargain and place someone else as the cost? Was it possible that Pa knew more than he was letting on?

A shiver of fear marched up Eliza's spine. Pa might say he'd never bargained, but he could be lying...couldn't he?

"Get ready for bed, Win," Eliza said, struggling to pry her fingers loose from where her nails had bitten tiny crescent moons into her palms.

They passed through the door that separated the restaurant from the back kitchen and living space, and there, shifted their three cots closer to the potbelly stove that would keep them warm through the night. In summer, they slept upstairs with the windows open to take advantage of Cape Fen's cool ocean breeze.

Eliza shook out Winnie's nightdress and smoothed the covers to her cot, finding the little wooden owl hidden beneath her pillow. Winnie dressed, climbed into bed, then ducked beneath the quilt.

"Would you still love me, if I looked like this?" Winnie yanked down the quilt fast, then shoved two fingers against her nose while two others two drew her cheeks down and two more pulled her mouth wide.

Eliza lost herself in a smile. "Sure, Winnie. I'd still love you if you kept your fingers in your mouth for the rest of your life. I'd love you no matter what."

Winnie cackled and lay back. Eliza tucked the ends of the moon-patterned quilt under her toes, under her calves and thighs, and under her back so she was cocooned in warmth on all sides. Then, Eliza crawled into her own bed. Nervousness churned in her belly and set her fingers to kneading the hem of her star-patterned quilt. Their mother had stitched Eliza and Winnie's quilts, a moon on one and a sun on the other, so that they would belong together in the sky.

You two are like that, their mother had whispered at night, pulling up covers to hug shoulders tight. *Best friends, soaring around in the heaven together.*

When you're little, Ma used to tell them, *play is your work. Play hard while you dream and play hard tomorrow after you wake. That's why I wanted two of you—two daughters to be best friends, to be the sun and the moon to dream together in the sky.* But now, their mother wasn't there to tuck them in, and so Eliza crushed her dreams and her memories of Ma beneath her angry fists.

She refused to play and to make believe like her mother once encouraged her to do. She had more important things to do, because it was beginning to look like someone had bargained away Winnie's life, and for all she knew, that someone had been Pa.

FIVE

—

*Colby Parlett dreamed. Slithering like a snake, she snuck along a tunnel, up through layers of caked dirt and frozen grass and thickened fog. Climbing a ladder with rungs made of starlight and crossing craters of glittering ice on the moon, she traveled on, not knowing where she went, only knowing that going some*where *was better than staying some*here.

Eliza battled sleep, dragging herself toward the surface of wakefulness. Fingers spread wide with thick skin pulled taut between bones, she pushed against water in the way her mother taught her.

Your legs do all the work. Your hands are there to act as paddles. Her mother's voice was a silent thing, words written into Eliza's muscles in such a way that she would never forget, even if she didn't want to remember.

It was hours upon hours—or was it days upon days?—until finally, her eyes opened to ghostly light inside the Fen Jester. While sleeping, she hadn't dreamed, didn't remember ever having dreamed, but for a moment, as she lay still with heavy bones weighed into her cot, she felt if she'd spent the night swimming against a tide.

Beside her, Winnie lay curled in a ball under the covers, having snuck beside her sometime during the night. *Alive and safe.* The current of anxiety that had swept through Eliza's veins faded, though still she felt it swishing in her depths, ready to rise. She woke Winnie, and they both dressed proper for the First Frost gathering—Cape Fen's yearly celebration of Baron Dire's return to their shores.

Winnie wore a muslin dress with ruffles at the wrists and neckline, over which Eliza made her wear a coat so she wouldn't get cold. Eliza wore a high-necked blouse tucked into a long skirt; something she'd taken from her mother's closet and altered so it fit her waist. She wasn't quite sure if she'd done it right, but at nearly twelve, she was supposed to lower the hemline of her skirt. Without a mother to ask though, she'd had to make guesses based on pictures she found in the Macy's catalog dropped off by the postman.

The whole town gathered in the middle of a wide park, smooth grass giving way to a bell tower at its center. The girls wore ribbons in their hair with ruffled dresses and high stockings, while their mothers wore hats fitted over their heads. Clean-shaven men wore suits and ties with long jackets layered over, with boys wearing warm knitwear. They were all dressed for a fancy party—*not* that Eliza considered this a party. If she were in charge, Baron Dire's return would be a mourning and everyone would wear black.

Pa dragged them through the gathering and toward the right side where the crowd thinned, finding a comfortable space to stand beside the Cape Fen welcome sign posted near the road. Dew slicked along white-painted letters which read a simple greeting: WELCOME TO CAPE FEN, WHERE DREAMS GROW.

In the center of the park stood Jarvis Bodfish, the Cape's lore-keeper and priest. White feathers circled his collar, the soft silken strands fluttering in the slight breeze. Once, Eliza had loved hearing the story Mr. Bodfish would tell, because her mother had loved it. But now, Eliza couldn't quite remember what it was that drew her in: the magic, the mystery, the love story… And so now, she had to listen in dismay as Mr. Bodfish spun the well-worn tale.

"I'm tired of waiting, Mr. Bodfish! Let's get this started," someone shouted from the crowd. Eliza peered around, not recognizing the voice until she spotted Lionel Parlett, her uncle. Colby stood beside her father. Unlit torch in one hand and ribbons streaming from the other, Lionel and Colby stood amid Eliza's Parlett side of the family, including Loretta Parlett, Kendare Lovell's widow.

Mr. Bodfish looked down at Lionel. "Are you going to be difficult, Parlett?"

"My family has had a very trying past twenty-four hours, Mr. Bodfish. You'll have to forgive us if we're impatient and ready to return home."

Mr. Bodfish's gaze shifted to Loretta, his face paling.

Loretta stood beside Lionel, her expression fierce despite the chapped, tear-stained skin beneath her eyes. "I wouldn't have missed this for the world," she said.

Eliza turned away from Loretta, unnerved at how closely she matched the vague shape of Ma in her memory. She hadn't often seen her aunt, but she knew when Loretta smiled, it took on a brittle shape, as if she'd practiced it before a mirror and hadn't found the trick to making it reach her eyes.

Mr. Bodfish began, "As our grandmothers and grandfathers told, and as lore now says, the first Dire Witch landed on Cape Fen just over one hundred years ago in 1811, bringing with her the frost of winter and the magic of the moon held within her one white-clouded eye. All was well until Baron Hawksmoor fell in love with the witch. 'I will do anything to be with you and have you love me in return,' he told her. And so the witch, being clever and brilliant at her work, struck with him a bargain. *Come to me in three nights wearing a cloak made of the fur of a wolf, a necklace of teeth, and rings with claws at the center, and then I will love you forever.* The man did as she asked, and in three days, he appeared at her door in the outfit she had requested."

"And she loved him forever and ever and ever," Colby muttered, just loud enough for those near to hear. "All because he'd dressed up like a fool."

Mr. Bodfish kept speaking, a strange tightness to his cheeks. "Yes, she did love him. Truly and forever. But only after she'd renamed herself Baroness Dire and transformed Hawksmoor into a wolf by the magic of the moon."

~

The magic of the moon; the magic of the moon, chattered Eliza's thoughts as she walked beside her sister. No one in the gathering spoke. At the front of the group, the elderly in town rode horse-drawn carts, leading everyone as they cut through low-hanging afternoon fog on Old Queen Mae, as silent and haunting as veiled ghosts. The procession headed down Old Queen Mae, passing by the library and courthouse, by the Hardwicks' shop, and by the Fen Jester. They walked through the center of town and out the other side, moving past closed-up shops, the fountain children threw wishes into during summer, the bookstore two stories high, the ice cream parlor, the Orpheum Theater where silent films from Hollywood played and comedy troupes performed in the summer, and the five-and-ten where Eliza bought dime novels, the penny biplane toy for Winnie, and Hershey's chocolate that Pa said would rot her teeth but that she ate all the same. They passed Landis's doctor's office with pies and cakes in the front window, sold by his wife, and the McMurry Bank where Mr. McMurry parked his new self-start Cadillac where everyone in town could admire it.

The closer they drew to their destination, the headier the scent of the ocean became. It gummed to Eliza's skin, as sticky as the remembered feel of her mother's embrace. They walked the entire time in silence, stopping at the crest of a beach covered by the same dark pebbles as Fen Bay. Lore said this was the beach on which Dire's witch-grandmother landed so long ago. Back then, the First Frost gathering was a true celebration, a welcoming party of sorts, meant to celebrate the magic of the Dire Witch... Things had been different back then. The first witch had been a proper witch, not at all like the witch's grandson, who was now in charge of the magic.

Come spring, Fenians would repeat the process but in reverse, sending off winter's thaw with wreaths made of early spring blossoms and shrimp spiced in peppers hot enough to melt the frost from their blood.

Sound rushed over them as they stood at the top of an embankment that led down to a long, wide beach. Ocean waves stretched upward to peel apart the clouds. They scraped at the sun as if to pull it under to heat its cold, depthless belly. But Eliza had swum beneath its surface, and she knew its liquid fingers to be liars—its waters were not so cold or heartless as the surface would have everyone believe on this dreary day. Beneath, there was life, there was…

Winnie tugged at her hand, and Eliza tore her gaze from the flickers of light against water.

"You're hurting my fingers," Winnie said.

Eliza loosened her hold on Win.

"I know we are weary," Mr. Bodfish said from somewhere to her left, "but it's time. Winter comes whether we ask it to or not. It's for us to find ways to survive. It's time." And he led them down to the beach.

Pa appeared at Eliza's side and placed one hand on her shoulder. A slight tremor quaked in his fingers.

"Are you okay?" Eliza asked.

He frowned in response, saying, "Keep track of your sister.

Don't get caught up in any of your Parlett cousins' shenanigans. You know how they are at gatherings." With that, he walked away with hands stuffed in his coat pockets.

On the beach, the Fenians freed the words they'd held during their walk, and the solemn group turned giddy, making the day feel like a jamboree.

"*Dire's ship came rolling in, rolling in, rolling in,*" Lionel Parlett sang. "*Dire's ship came rolling in, in one fine morning!*"

The rest of the Parletts joined in, until the entire crowd sang the tune:

"*She brought to us a magic curse, a magic curse, a magic curse. She brought to us a magic curse that keeps us from ever leaving. We bargain away our very lives, our very lives, our very lives. We bargain away our very lives to gain the things we dream of.*"

With the rollicking tune as her backdrop, Eliza didn't go in search of Winnie—she'd already spotted her playing in the sand. Instead, she snuck after Pa. She squeezed between the revelers, those who'd pulled food from picnic baskets filled with bite-size fried oysters, fish filets topped with goat cheese and wrapped in soft flour shells, lobster stuffed inside hard rolls, and fried dough Mrs. Landis made just that morning, still warm and soft in the center.

Pa stopped walking when he reached Lionel Parlett, one of the people Eliza had been told to stay far, far away from.

Nervous energy shivered through her. She ducked low and circled behind Pa and Lionel. She ended up at the water-softened sand where waves crawled up the beach.

"Something's happening... What do you know... Tell me—" Pa's words melded with the surf, and Eliza scooted beneath a lifeguard stand to hide.

"*Now* you want my help?" Lionel asked. "After four years of silence and refusal? You're trying to make a mockery of me, Waylon, and the day after my brother-in-law's death too."

"I am sorry about that, but you know the cost of bargaining better than anyone. If Kendare bargained, he knew what might happen."

"No one bargains thinking they'll die, though sometimes that's exactly what happens," Lionel hissed. "You didn't accept my help after Tynne left."

"The only help you offered was to take in the girls, and that wasn't help I was willing to accept. You did nothing to try and get Tynne back, to find where she went."

Eliza clutched her arms around her legs. Pa never spoke about her mother, *never*.

Lionel grabbed Pa's arm, but Pa twisted free and said, "I've never cared about the way your family conducted their business, but she hated you and so I hated you. She never would have forgiven me had I sent the girls to live with you."

Lionel's grin froze. Wildness entered his eyes.

"I didn't come to talk about her. I didn't want to bring up the past," Pa said.

"Past, present, future—it's *always* connected."

"You're eavesdropping," said a voice right beside Eliza's ear.

Eliza leapt, rolling backward to find Colby seated criss-crossed beside her.

"I'm not," Eliza whispered, even as she realized how stupid the lie must seem.

Colby said, "I'm not going to tattle on you, if that's what you're worried about. Every good Parlett knows that eavesdropping is sometimes the best way to learn things."

"I'm not a Parlett."

"You're half Parlett. That's enough. We've all got dreams in us, and sometimes those dreams make us do sneaky things during the day."

"I don't dream." Eliza steeled herself against her cousin's tricky way of talking. "What do you want?" she said.

"You're jumpier than normal." Colby watched her father as she spoke, glossy eyes tracking the sharp way Lionel moved. "Does it have to do with the Wolf? I'm assuming you've never been close to it, not like you were yesterday."

"And you have?"

"Of course."

Surprise locked Eliza's muscles in place.

"All Parletts have. Meeting Baron Dire and seeing his Wolf is like a rite of passage."

Eliza knew of no one else for whom it was a rite of passage to meet Baron Dire. The Serlings might be banned from anything to do with Dire or his Wolf, but of course the very opposite would be encouraged for the Parletts. *Of course.*

Colby watched Lionel as he responded to Eliza's pa. Eliza had lost track of their conversation.

"Our dads went to school together, you know?" Colby continued. "Once, your dad knocked out my dad's front teeth."

"He did not!"

"Maybe not, but my dad said he did. He likes to rewrite stories though, so who knows what really happened."

Eliza couldn't fit this tale into her picture of her pa. She'd never seen him raise his fists in anger. She drew up her knees and thought to ask Colby about Dire, about bargains, about the Wolf, but years of distrust sewn by her parents kept those questions bottled up tight.

Instead, she said, "I hate the Wolf's origin story." Because she did, and because she knew Colby did too.

"It's the worst. I always figure that love isn't so simple as a spell, like the story says. Besides, Mr. Bodfish always leaves out the good stuff." Colby paused, eyes narrowing at a point down the beach. "*Ugh*. My stupid brother and sister are trying to light something on fire." She crawled under a beam of the lifeguard's post. But before she left, she said, "If you feel like telling me why the Wolf has you so upset, you know where to find me," and then turned to walk along the sand.

"Colby!" Eliza hissed.

Her cousin faced her, though she still walked backward.

"Is there a way to discover what someone might have bargained?"

"There's no way for certain. What's between Dire and a bargainer stays between them."

Eliza's fingers sunk into the sand, skin scraping against hard pebbles and sharp stones. She'd hoped Colby would know of a way to discover what bargain Winnie was part of, to know what someone might have written into a deal with Dire.

Colby spun and broke into a jog, heading toward her siblings. Only moments later, a lifeguard's post some hundred yards away flared to life, bright yellow flame crawling over the wooden stand. No one on the beach quite seemed to care. It burned, a pyre set in winter's honor.

"You don't know what I would do!" Pa's voice dragged her attention back to his conversation with Lionel. "You have no idea what I would do to find where she went. *You have no idea!*"

Sudden anger lit inside Eliza, as quick and hot as the

Parletts' bonfire. Pa had never done *anything* to look for Ma! He'd let her row away from their family on a boat, somehow crossing over Fen's barrier and disappearing onto the mainland. Then *he'd* gone and disappeared into his grief-filled work in Ma's shed out back behind the Jester, leaving Eliza to pick up the pieces of their family alone. By herself. At eight.

Either Pa was lying to Lionel, or he was lying to himself.

Colby might not have been any help, but maybe Eliza had the answer right in front of her. Maybe Pa *had* done something to find Ma that Eliza didn't know about, and the only *something* too shameful for anyone else to know would have been a bargain with Dire.

"What would you do to find Ma?" Eliza whispered, her voice covered up by the waves. "What did you do?"

SIX

Miss Alayna dreamed. No breeze rumpled Fen Bay's
surface, its waters forming a mirror.
"You promised to make all my dreams come true,"
she said to the image in its surface. One black eye
and one clouded eye stared back at her.

It was late afternoon by the time they returned home. Pa hauled Winnie up by her armpits and tossed her over his shoulders, then spun in a circle, sending her into a fit of shrieking giggles. Eliza watched from where she sat on her sleeping cot, a forced smile pasted to her mouth. She couldn't stop hearing what Pa had said: *You have no idea what I would do to find where she went.*

Had Pa been lying earlier when he'd said he hadn't bargained? Had he become so desperate to find Ma that he'd asked Dire for help? She'd been gone for four years. What if he'd bargained away Winnie's life for a chance to get Ma back?

Worse, how could Eliza believe this of him? He might not be perfect, but he was still her pa. Suspicion and confusion simmering inside her, she unbuttoned her coat and lay it on the bed beside her.

Pa set Winnie down, who stumbled with dizziness before plopping on the floor. He said, "I'm going to the shed." He ruffled Winnie's hair, and then disappeared out the Jester's back door.

This was Eliza's chance, when she was too upset about what he might have done to Winnie to second-guess the consequences of confronting him.

"Stay inside," she murmured to Winnie.

"Well I *was* planning on visiting the moon," Winnie muttered.

Eliza followed Pa out back. There, partly hidden by a tall row of pines, stood Ma's shed. Its tin roof sloped at a sharp angle, out of place among the Cape-style homes and their carefully shingled roofs.

She opened the door and was hit by the sharp scent of wood. Of herbs. Of medicine. Of the items that went into creating the sleeping draught that had become more important than his family. Pa's sadness lived here.

Eliza's own sadness was wispy. She often tried to grasp hold of it but could never quite dig her fingers in tight enough. Standing beside the bookshelves that lined the wall, she fingered the spines of the books as she waited for Pa to appear from the back of the two-room shed. *Secrets of Herbs* stood beside *Medicinal Properties of Dreaming-Plants,* which was propped against *Herbs for the Tea Connoisseur* and rested near *One Hundred Myths of Magic* and *A Short History of Cape Fen.*

Pa had gifted each of these to Ma. In fact, he'd built the entire shed for her right after their wedding. Once, this had been Ma's special place, though she'd always invited Eliza and Winnie inside while she made sleeping draughts and tonics for the people of Fen. Now that she was gone, Pa carried on her work, though it had taken him over in a way it'd never taken over Ma.

His clomping steps drew near, echoing from the back as he made his way through the workspace. He stood to the side of a barrel, maneuvering cans of some liquid or another. Leaning close, his nose flared as he smelled the contents.

Questions crowded her thoughts: the sleeping draughts he worked on, Winnie, bargains, Dire, *Ma.*

"Shouldn't you be getting ready to go with your Aunt Zilpha?" Pa said without looking up.

She started. The questions in her mind strewed about as if they were leaves blown away by a sharp, unexpected wind. "Go with her where?" Zilpha was the only Parlett sibling of Ma's that Pa came close to trusting, if only for the fact that when she was young, she'd moved off the Parlett lands—same as Ma—and had never returned.

"She called early this morning. She's taking you with her to work this afternoon—she should be here soon. I told you before we headed out."

"No, you didn't."

"I'm sure I did."

"No! I was planning on taking Winnie to the library this afternoon."

"Well, I told someone that Zilpha called."

"Winnie? Did you tell Winnie?"

He finally looked up from the pieces of grain he'd counted out in his palm. "I thought I told you."

Pa couldn't tell the difference between his daughters. Or didn't care who was who. Or was too distracted to know. Or was oblivious to the goings on around him. Or...

One, two, three. She held her breath as anxiety slid through her.

Four, five, six. Her lungs strained. Calm spread through her, and—

"Stop!" Pa slammed his grain-filled palm against the side of a barrel.

Eliza's eyes widened. Her body froze. She didn't exhale.

Pa pointed at her. "Eliza Tynne Serling, don't you dare do that."

Tears trembled onto her eyelashes. Her middle name echoed inside the shed not once or twice, but three times. She knew without thinking that it was the first time in almost four years that Pa had said Ma's name, and now, he'd said her name in irritation toward Eliza.

"*Eliza.*" Worry crumpled the crow's feet at the edges of Pa's eyes, but it was too late. Her tears had already begun. "It's a strange habit, Eliza. Holding your breath is—well, it's strange. I'm sorry. *I'm sorry.*"

Eliza finally breathed, a small slip of air through her nose, noiseless so Pa wouldn't hear. Ma'd been the one to teach her to hold her breath when scared, when worried, when needing calm, and Pa hated that she still kept the habit.

Eliza thrummed with embarrassment. "I'll get ready for Zilpha," she said. Then she bolted, running into the Jester to the sight of Winnie standing on her tiptoes to reach the ringing telephone.

"Hello? Oh. Hi, Mr. Filemon's pa. Okay, bye." Winnie dropped the receiver to dangle at the end of the cord. "He's talking to some man," she said to Eliza and scrambled beneath one of the Jester's round tables with her wooden owl.

Eliza hung up the phone for her short sister and crouched beside Winnie.

Winnie stuck her head out from under a chair. "You look bad."

"Gee, thanks, Win." Eliza scrubbed at her face, trying to erase any tear tracks that might exist. "Zilpha's coming to pick me up. I'm supposed to clean houses with her today."

"Pa told me she was coming. I want to go too."

"Whenever you try and help us clean, you double the work I have to do because you fog up the windows and draw shapes in them." Eliza ran trembling fingers over Winnie's hair. The love she felt for Win expanded inside her. She swallowed back her feelings and said, "Stay here and play with your owl. Read to it. Have fun. Promise me you'll stay inside. You *can't* go out at night, not with the Wolf around. Promise you won't."

"I'm not scared of the Wolf."

I'm scared for you, she thought, though out loud, she said, "Don't go anywhere."

Eliza kissed Winnie on the forehead, then grabbed her coat and headed into the day where the sun hung low in the sky; the First Frost gathering had run long this year. She stood in the middle of Old Queen Mae with her hands stuffed into her pockets and her chin tucked into the popped collar of her wool coat.

The cough and rumble of an engine rattled down Old Queen Mae Street. Zilpha's motorcar blasted through the middle of the road just a hair too fast, and when Zilpha slammed on the brakes, the tail of the vehicle weaved back and forth. Eliza jumped out of the way just in time—the back tires slipped and the motorcar slid straight over the point where she'd stood.

"You almost just killed me!" Eliza shouted, heart thumping too hard, as if it wanted to shake loose from her body and go somewhere Zilpha couldn't run over it. "You almost just killed me, and I can't go dying, Zilpha. There's too much to do—keeping Win safe and making sure Pa doesn't forget to eat and surviving winter and…and…and besides, I can't remember the last time I dusted the Jester!" she said, thinking of her mother's stained-glass lamp and the sheen of dust that covered its innards.

"Dusting?" Zilpha Parlett raised her eyebrows. She hung her head out over the driver's side door, wisps of black hair jutting out from her scalp in every direction. "You in a mood today? Cause that was quite an earful you just gave me."

"You almost ran me over."

"Then thank goodness you have such fast reflexes!" Zilpha thumped the side of her car. Her leather driving gloves were covered in a thin film of dirt kicked up by gravel roads. "Are you planning on getting in, or are we going to sit here in the cold?

Because if we wait much longer, the motor will stall and you'll have to turn the crank."

"I'm not strong enough," Eliza said, eyeing the place where a hand crank fitted to the front of the car made the engine turn. It was true she couldn't pull the handle hard enough to start the car, but it was even more true that she didn't want to die—she'd read in the newspaper that over on the continent, a car had backfired, causing the crank to whack a man right in the head, killing him.

Eliza climbed in the passenger side, boosting herself up onto the seat. She shifted around a bit, avoiding the place on the right side where a metal spring had popped loose and poked against the fabric of the bench. Zilpha slammed one bare foot into the gas pedal. She never wore shoes. Not even in winter. The tires squealed, and they skidded into motion.

Zilpha shouted over the roar of the engine, "Got keys in the glove box to a place I think you'll find interesting."

"What house is it?"

"It's a surprise. I think you'll like it."

They flew west on Old Queen Mae, heading through town. They passed by the Hardwicks' store and the schoolhouse and came up on the place where the road passed by the park and bell tower. A lone man sat hunched in the center of the tower. They drove past, and when he looked up, Eliza saw it was Mr. Chess.

Five years ago, Mr. Chess had disappeared, and twelve months later he'd returned, walking across Fen Bay's beach the day after the First Frost gathering. He couldn't remember a single thing about the vanished year of his life. Sheriff Olavi had looked into the disappearance, but from what Eliza remembered, nothing was ever discovered. Yet another strange happening on Fen.

Zilpha increased her speed. A glass panel blocked the wind at the front of the motorcar, but no wraparound closed in the rest of the vehicle, which meant that the cold whipped around them. Zilpha stuck her arm out the driver's side door, cupped one hand, and let it take the flight of a bird in the wind. Eliza tucked her hands inside her coat and hunched down to stay warm, the air cutting straight through her skin.

After about ten minutes of driving, the road split. Old Queen Mae continued west and crossed over the bridge that connected the Cape to the continent, and beneath it ran a small channel that ships sailed through. The left fork of the road turned into Highway 24 which curved back east along the southern coast of the Cape. This road was what vacationers called a "scenic highway," running thirty miles all the way from the Cape's shoulder to its bent elbow and up to the very tip of the peninsula. Zilpha drove toward the split, drawing near to the place over which Fenians couldn't cross. Mainlanders thought Fenians odd, that they didn't leave because they chose it, when the truth was much worse; this was as close to the mainland as Fenians could get, and even this nearness to the bridge became painful.

Eliza braced herself. The first wave came in a pinching of her lungs. The second in a narrowing of her vision. The third in a fuzz at the back of her skull. The world smelled of the lightning storm three years ago, when bolts struck Fen, setting sections of town ablaze.

They didn't cross the bridge. Zilpha clutched the wheel and pressed harder on the gas pedal. They flew, taking the left turn that led them back east along the highway. Pain zipped through Eliza, and her chin fell to her chest. This wasn't like holding her breath—she was good at that. This was like having the breath sucked from her, *stolen* from her.

Little by little, the farther Zilpha drove from the bridge, Eliza's thoughts flooded back.

"We couldn't have taken the back roads?" she said when she felt able to speak without gasping.

"This way's shorter, and I like driving the pavement better than the gravel."

"The other way doesn't want me dead," Eliza said, grumpiness making her tongue sharp.

"You're just like your mother. She always complained about this route as well. It's never bothered me to be reminded of exactly how trapped we are."

Eliza's toes curled inside her shoes and fingers curled into fists, and she turned away from Zilpha to look out the window.

"You *are* like her, you know. I miss her too," Zilpha said. "It's all right if you miss her. Sometimes, I wonder if we might see her again."

Eliza squashed flat the dream of seeing her mother again and said, "Never." She already knew the answer to the question of when Ma might return.

The flat, rich earth, deep woods, and rock-strewn beaches of lower Fen gave way to rolling hills, sharp cliffs, and blue-pebbled beaches of upper Fen—a place people liked to call Rio. Mansions rose out of the late afternoon gloom, lining up close to one another and overlooking the rough ocean. During the winter, Rio was a ghost town, just like the old mining towns in Colorado Eliza had read about but would never have the chance to visit.

During summer, Zilpha ran a taxi service for the rich people who needed to be driven around on their vacations, but in winter, she cleaned the empty mansions of Rio while their owners were away. Often, she asked Eliza to help, paying her five whole pennies for an hour's work.

They drove through Rio, heading toward the easternmost edge of the Cape where surf spray clouded the sky. Here, they didn't face Fen Bay, but rather faced the wide-open ocean that stretched to the east. Eliza sat up in her seat, ignoring the broken spring in the cushion even though it poked against the back of her leg.

At last, Zilpha brought them to a stop.

"Oh," Eliza said. "Here? We're cleaning *here*?"

"Lighthouses need cleaning too." Zilpha parked the motorcar and peeled off her driving gloves, exchanging them for a key stashed in the glove box.

Eliza got out and gazed up. The white-and-red-striped structure came to a point at the top, and there, a cone of clearpaned glass glistened. Since the lighthouse had been abandoned years before, no keeper currently lived in it.

"Stop gawping and get your gear." Zilpha swung out of the motorcar and reached into the back seat to pull out a case of cleaning supplies.

Eliza reached into the back too and carried out a second, smaller set. She held the case by its handle and clenched her hand tight, trying to still the nervous jitters that ticked through her fingers.

"You coming or no?" Zilpha already had one foot in the front door of the small home that was connected to the lighthouse. Her pants were rolled up past her calves, revealing her bare feet that disappeared inside in the next moment.

"But this is—"

The front door slammed behind Zilpha.

"Baron Dire's lighthouse," Eliza finished.

SEVEN

*Zilpha Parlett dreamed. Her bare toes curled through
dead, prickly grass, digging at the hard dirt and
feeling small vibrations in the ground. How far
could elephants hear through the earth? Six miles?
She could hear Cape Fen through her feet, but all
she wanted was to know if her nieces were safe.*

All Eliza could think as she stood on the stoop was that
her feet now walked the same place Baron Dire's feet
had walked before. Baron Dire, who freely bargained away the
lives of Cape Fen's occupants. What was it all those people had

bargained for? Was it worth it? Somehow, it must have been, or else why would the town continue to bargain? Clearly, no one could win against Dire.

One, two, three. She drowned her feelings beneath the held breath in her lungs and the silent numbers in her head. She couldn't do anything now but pretend bravery, and so she stepped inside.

The lighthouse was spare of decorations. A small wooden table and two chairs sat in the middle of a kitchen, with a potbelly stove directly behind it. One door stood closed on the far end of the room, and toward the opposite side of the house, winding stairs led up and up and up to the light far above. Only one electric bulb dangled from the ceiling, illuminating a deck of cards that rested on the table. The cards were patterned with the face of a wolf, just like the deck of cards Zilpha kept in her motorcar. The first card was flipped over; the black Queen of Spades gleamed up at Eliza. She reached out to trace the queen's face—

Thump.

She snatched back her hand and cast her gaze about the house. Zilpha's shadowed form didn't appear on the stairs. *Thump,* the sound came again, this time from behind the closed door.

Thump.

Eliza crept across the floor, sneaking just the same way she did when playing hide-and-seek with Winnie in the woods in summer. She pressed her fingertips to the door. It swung open, hinges groaning against a lack of use. She turned on the light.

"Ahh!" Zilpha shouted and tossed an arm up, covering her eyes while tottering on a chair.

Eliza's heartbeat scurried against her ribs. The blinding imprint of Zilpha standing on a chair, changing a lightbulb high overhead was seared into her eyes.

"The first bulb's fine, but the second's blown," Zilpha said. "I'll have to run back out with a new one tomorrow. *Catch.*"

Eliza snatched the bulb out of the air and cradled it against her belly to keep it from falling and shattering against the ground.

"Still quick on your feet. Good, good," Zilpha said. "Now get to cleaning. The windows way up top need to be scrubbed."

Eliza huffed out an annoyed breath of air and backed away with the lightbulb clasped in one hand. She slipped it inside the pocket of her coat and headed up the back stairs. Of course, she'd been with Zilpha inside lighthouses—there were seven working lighthouses on the Cape altogether—and had cleaned their windows before. They were major tourist attractions in the summer. Something about the steady lights as they swung through the black of night hypnotized people. Late evening, you could drive by the lighthouse beaches and count the people lined up, standing huddled together against the salty breeze, watching the beam of light and listening to waves wash against the beach.

But despite all the lighthouses she'd visited, Eliza had never stepped foot inside Baron Dire's. For all she knew, no one had... except for Zilpha.

Eliza climbed the stairs, all fifty-seven of them, and then crawled up a short ladder to the very top floor. Dire's lighthouse had been retired by the coast guard years before. It stood at a precarious angle against the cliff, close enough that they worried it would tumble into the ocean sometime in the next decade. Because of this, the uppermost floor remained empty, though the glass panes still needed to be maintained. Once on the top level, her feet rooted into the floor. The windows of the lighthouse were hazy with salt spray, but still, it was clear enough, and she pressed her palm against a pane to see the ocean beyond. The endless waters swept out and away, stretching across her line of sight.

Eliza stood in place, unable to move. Distantly, she heard Zilpha call and say she was going to check on repairs outside of the lighthouse. The front door closed. The cool glass beneath her palm fogged with the heat of her skin, and she pressed her forehead against it.

One, two, three. This was the world Ma had taught her to love—the one with ribbons of water connecting one side of the Earth to the other.

Thirty-seven, thirty-eight, thirty-nine. The one Ma had let her dive beneath to touch the ocean floor with her fingertips.

Forty-five, forty-six, forty-seven. The one Eliza hadn't dared swim in for four years.

Eliza unlatched a small lock on one of the windows and swung it outward. Wisps of fog trailed in, bringing with it the scent of sand caught between toes and salt crusted to fingertips and hair tugged free from braids by the wind. She stepped onto the small, iron balcony that rounded the lighthouse and forcefully turned from the ocean, setting out to clean the windows. She went through rag after rag, wiping away the grime and muck from the lighthouse. Her arms ached from scrubbing, and her calves cramped from standing on her toes. Breathless, she threw her last rag inside the lighthouse and turned back to the ever-darkening ocean to rest.

Salt spray misted her cheeks. Her heart tugged. *She missed this.*

Not knowing how long she stood there, only knowing she could watch the waves forever, she saw the moment the sun fully disappeared in the west and day's light winked out.

She shoved herself away from the glass. How had so much time passed? She scanned the grounds for Zilpha, but her gaze snagged on the darkened beach. Something glinted against the sand. Two eerie glowing dots flickered in and out of view, almost the same color as the moon. Her heartbeat grew loud in her ears, and her lungs began to ache. She let out the air from her chest on a slow, steady stream through her nose.

The beach had stood empty and now…it didn't.

The Wolf prowled along the beach, right at the water's edge. Fear froze her limbs. She'd seen the moment of time between disappearance and existence, the moment when the moon took over the sky and the Wolf had come into being. The fear didn't exist *for* her, but for Winnie. For the sister she had nearly lost. Had the Wolf leapt a second earlier, Winnie would've—*no*. Eliza refused to think of it. Instead, she shook herself loose of the fear and allowed in her anger.

By the light of the moon, Eliza saw the Wolf lift its muzzle to the wind. After a long moment, it turned to lope down the beach.

Every bit of frustration Eliza had felt during the day—at Pa, at the Parletts, at Dire and his bargains, at secrets, at *Ma*—drew her tight. Her hands rounded into fists, and her heartbeat lit like kindling.

She would do anything for Winnie, and the Wolf—this moonlit, magicked *thing*—didn't want her, because no matter what, the Wolf always had a reason for attacking. No one had bargained with Eliza as the price. The certainty of this made her reckless.

She bolted down the stairs almost too fast to control and tossed her cleaning kit on the table, where two Queen of Spades now stared up at her. She ran out the front door and around to the back, to the place where the ledge looked over a sharp cliff.

She spied the Wolf stalking the beach. From the top of the lighthouse, she'd noticed a set of wooden stairs that led to the sand below, and she hurriedly searched for them now. Finding the first step marked by a large rock, she started down as fast as her legs would allow, until her feet sank into the soft, pebbly sand at the bottom of the steps. She ran, minuscule stones scattering over her shoes and beneath her socks, rubbing at her skin. Eliza traced the Wolf's paw prints that were set into the wet sand, noting the sharp claw marks and the pads that pressed beneath the Wolf's weight.

A ghost wolf, Winnie had said.

But the Wolf stood up the beach, monstrous and shadowed and real. It faced her.

You have nothing to be scared of, she told herself.

Not her. *Not her. NOT*—"Leave my sister alone!" she shouted.

The Wolf cocked its head.

Her throat ached with the force of her yell. "She didn't make a bargain!"

Its lips tugged back.

"Baron Dire has no right to her life!"

It began to run. *Toward* Eliza. Cutting through the sand as easy as teeth through fruit ice pops on hot summer days.

Adrenaline raced through Eliza. She braced. *It's not coming for me. It's not.* But the sight of the thundering Wolf heading toward her was too much to bear. She turned and ran.

Sand squelched behind her. Panting breaths drew near. Eliza reached the bottom of the stairs. A growl ripped through the air, and she took the first step, tripped and fell, hitting her shins. She turned, one arm braced over her face. Her opposite hand grasped at her pocket, at the lightbulb that had miraculously stayed whole. A shadow fell over her. She dragged the bulb free and chucked it into the air. The Wolf leapt and snapped at the light. It shattered, dusting its snout in glass and filaments. A furious roar hurtled from its throat, and a hard force smacked into her—*crack*! Her head hit the stairs, and a shroud of black fell over her vision. She blinked furiously, trying to regain the sight she'd lost, but then the Wolf's heated body was there, standing above her.

Snuff, snuff. The Wolf pressed its nose into the too-thin skin of her neck.

Her vision peeled open, the world returning from the inside out, as if she were exiting from a long, narrow tunnel. The Wolf's coat filled her sight.

Snuff, snuff. It inhaled her scent.

"No, no, *no*," Eliza chant-whispered.

A low howling whine started in its throat, and something responded inside Eliza. A ball of twine wrapped around her throat and drew outward, heaving a piece of her off-kilter. The Wolf's song intensified—

A sharp whistle cut through the night.

The Wolf backed away.

But for the automatic inhalation of air into her lungs, Eliza's muscles were locked tight. She couldn't loosen them to stand, to move, to run. *Alive. I am alive. I am not dead. I am not eaten.* The refrain beat through her in a staccato rhythm, while the rest of her thoughts whirled and spun.

"And who are you?" said a voice down the beach, though she didn't dare look to discover who.

Before her, the Wolf's nostrils flared, and with its golden eyes hidden behind closed lids, it scented the air, probably searching for Winnie.

EIGHT

—

Filemon Hardwick dreamed. He stood on the middle of a pirate ship, sword in hand, shouting as the tentacles of a sea monster rose from the depths. Here, no one told him what to do. He was in control of his own story. This was adventure. This was fun. This was much better than real life.

Zilpha appeared above Eliza on the stairs.

"*Heh!*" Zilpha shouted and flicked both hands at the Wolf. "Be gone!"

The Wolf dropped low with ears tucked close to its head and lips pulled back in a snarl.

"Don't be cruel to my Wolf," said the voice on the beach.

"Don't be letting your Wolf eat my niece." Zilpha stalked down the steps, her bare feet taking her past Eliza as if she weren't there at all, as if the Wolf didn't stand close with teeth bared.

"Hello, Zilpha." The man drew near and beckoned to his Wolf, which went to meet him with head slunk down.

Eliza braced herself as she looked up at Dire, meeting at last the man who'd made it possible for her ma to leave. His melodic voice pitched deeper than she would've expected, reminding her of wind chimes. She was struck at how normal he appeared, and yet something strange glimmered about him, moonlight huddling around his shoulders like the silver clasps of a cape.

"Hello, Dire. You took your time in getting here this year, didn't you?" Zilpha said.

Baron Dire laughed, the stiff set of his shoulders loosening. "Rough waters stalled my travels."

"Our summer ran hot and long, so you stayed away. You think I don't know you?"

"No, I rather think you do. That's the problem."

Zilpha held Dire's gaze. A zip of energy Eliza didn't understand passed between them. Eliza tried to track it, looking from one to the other, but only became more confused the more she tried to decipher their carefully set stances.

At last, Zilpha said, "I wish you would've stayed away."

"You know that's not an option. All the same, I've missed you." Dire dropped his gaze, the slimness of his body falling into deeper shadow when he turned to the side. Eliza couldn't see the details of his face, and this bothered her. *One black and the other clouded and white*, lore said of Dire's eyes, like something of the moon lived inside him.

"You should stay indoors at night," he said to Eliza.

"You shouldn't send your Wolf to attack and kill," Eliza said, pressing her hands hard into the uneven steps beneath her, slivers of wood pricking against her skin.

"My Wolf doesn't kill. If a bargain someone's made ends in their death, that's their fault, not the fault of my Wolf."

One, two, three. Eliza pressed her tongue against the back of her teeth. She stilled the words that trampled through her head.

Dire watched her, pulling one gloved hand out of his pocket and rubbing the Wolf's fur between the shoulder blades. It tipped its head back, nose reaching nearly to his armpit.

"Eliza, go back to the lighthouse," Zilpha said.

Eliza uncurled her body from the stairs, the anger inside her feeling hot as summer sand blistered by the sun. She focused hard on not tripping up the steps back to the lighthouse. There, on the edge of the cliff, beside the large rock that marked the start to the stairway, Eliza lay on her belly with her chin set on folded arms and her ear tilted into the evening breeze. This, after all, was how sound worked—it *soared*.

"Have you decided on another bargain then?" Dire said.

A jolt passed through Eliza. *Zilpha had bargained before?* She clawed her fingers into the soft earth.

"No bargain," Zilpha said, "just a simple transaction—"

"What do you think bargains are, but a transaction of magic for a wish?"

Zilpha paused, and Eliza imagined her posture changing into one with legs braced wide. "You owe me payment for cleaning your lighthouse. That's all I need right now."

"I never contracted you for that job."

"That's not my problem."

Dire's sigh got snatched up in the wind, but still, Eliza heard it. It was filled with long-suffering, the same sort of noise Ma used to make when Pa trampled muddy work boots across the kitchen floor after midsummer rains.

Dire said, "I'll pay after you come and clean my home. I haven't been able to settle in for the monstrous amount of dust that descended during summer. My windows are grubby."

Zilpha snorted, then started up the stairs, taking two-at-a-time by the sound of it.

"And when you come," Dire said, "bring the girl with you."

Zilpha stilled, her next footfall not landing. "What do you want with Eliza?"

"Oh, it's not what I want with her, it's what *she* wants with *me*. I'm curious to find out."

Zilpha didn't reply and didn't offer warnings for Dire to stay away from Eliza. She should tell him to stay away, and the fact that she didn't caused Eliza to become even more suspicious than she already was.

She dared to peer over the edge of the cliff, dry grass tickling the soft underside of her jaw. Dire walked down the beach, and after him prowled his Wolf. Aided by the nearly full moon, their shadows stretched long and danced on the waves. She watched, shoving away the feeling that they took some part of her with them as they went.

"You heard?" Zilpha stood behind Eliza. She squished her toes into the same grass on which Eliza lay.

Eliza captured a lie between her teeth—obviously she'd been spying. Glad to have Colby's words as an excuse, she said, "I'm half Parlett, and every good Parlett knows that eavesdropping is sometimes the best way to learn things."

Zilpha let out a bark of laughter and stretched out a hand to help Eliza up.

"I'm going to help clean Dire's home?"

"I won't force you."

"But I can come?"

Zilpha raised one eyebrow. A small smile played on her mouth, quirking at the corners, until Eliza had to wonder if this was what her aunt had intended from the start.

I miss her too, you know, Zilpha had said. *Sometimes, I wonder if we might see her again.*

Have you decided on another bargain then? Dire had asked. Zilpha had refused tonight, but at one time, she hadn't. Eliza had assumed Pa had bargained away Winnie to try and find Ma, but Zilpha might be the one to blame.

NINE

Baron Dire didn't dream. Fear scrabbled at the edges of his mind, pulling upright the small hairs along the back of his neck. He distracted himself, sitting with the Wolf before the fire, eating lobster bisque, and playing a game of solitaire. But all the while, he felt as if something watched him...except no, the heavy drapes over the living room windows were pulled tight. Surely the tricky dreaming moon couldn't see him from where it hung in the sky.

Zilpha's motorcar puttered down the road leading from the lighthouse. They headed into the night, and Eliza almost asked her to turn back because she'd forgotten something important at the lighthouse of the beach. She patted her pockets, checking to see what she might have missed. But no, she'd brought nothing with her, and so there was nothing for her to have left behind. The feeling intensified. It felt as if something inside her had been knocked out of place by a hard force.

Once at the Jester, Zilpha walked her inside. A few bowls sat on the tables, licked nearly clean by the customers who'd stopped by in the evening. During winter, Pa usually kept the Jester closed. They made enough money three seasons of the year to last the fourth. But sometimes, he opened the restaurant on Friday and Saturday and served stew or chili to those interested.

"Sheriff Olavi called around," Pa said to Zilpha as he picked up bowls and brought them to the kitchen. "Doctor Landis ruled Kendare's death a drowning."

"But I saw Kendare," Eliza said, confused. "He hadn't been in the ocean. He hadn't been swimming."

"A person can drown in four inches of water," said Zilpha.

"What about the Wolf? There were paw prints beside his body!"

Zilpha said, "Sheriff Olavi has to put something official on the papers. You have to understand, authorities on the mainland won't accept 'bargain' as a cause of death."

"Death by *Wolf*! We already know how he died. He made a bargain, and the Wolf came for him, and now he's dead."

Pa and Zilpha exchanged a glance, one that made Eliza mad because she didn't know how to read it.

"Sheriff Olavi also said that Loretta Parlett decided to hold Kendare's funeral on Monday. School'll be canceled again," Pa said.

Eliza wrapped her arms around herself. She didn't want to go to Kendare's funeral. It made her feel strange, knowing he was a part of her family that she'd hardly known, and knowing too that he'd died in a way nobody wanted to talk about. She looked up at Pa, asking, "Is Winnie already in bed?"

He puffed out his cheeks, then let out the breath in one gust, before admitting, "Your sister climbed a tree and is refusing to come down."

Eliza's arms fell to her side, and she started toward the back door. "It's night out! The Wolf could be out there." Did Pa *want* her to get eaten? Did he want a second funeral after Kendare's? How could he leave her up there?

"She's safe enough," Pa said. "She'll come down when she decides."

Zilpha added, "Wolves can't climb trees."

Eliza ran out of the house and into the backyard. She'd seen the Wolf on the beach not even an hour ago! Surely it could be here, now. Why did no one else care what happened to Winnie?

"*Winnie!*" she shouted, scanning the dark trees for her sister. "Get yourself out of whatever tree it is you've climbed up!"

"I was bored," Winnie's voice floated down to her. "You were gone, and Pa wasn't paying me any attention, and I tried playing games, but nothing was fun."

"So you got yourself stuck in a tree?" Eliza said, locating Winnie at last up the bare branches of an oak tree.

"I'm not stuck. It's a very wonderful tree, and it's kept me company." Winnie patted the trunk.

Eliza reached up to the branch above her, discovering it was nearly out of her reach. Her sister was a squirrel to have climbed it so easily.

"School's canceled Monday," Eliza called up to her.

Winnie's small voice said, "Pa overheard on the party line that Miss Alayna was angry."

"Gossip," Eliza said. "She can't be angry over a funeral."

Winnie shifted her weight on the branch. "Bri will come back for Miss Alayna, won't he? She's having his baby."

Eliza's thoughts fell to Filemon, who always wore Bri's coat as if Bri were dead and not just disappeared to the continent to go to university. "I think, sometimes, babies can be complicated. Besides, Miss Alayna can't leave the Cape, and if I were Bri, I'd be worried about getting stuck in Fen if I came back. I'd be too scared to try."

The back door of the Jester slammed shut, and Pa and Zilpha's voices reached them.

"Get down, would you? Zilpha's here, and we need to get inside. You know the Wolf comes out at night." Eliza held up her hands.

"I'm scared, Eliza." Winnie's voice trembled, but in a fake, laughing sort of way.

"You know you're not allowed to lie in our house," Eliza said.

"We aren't in our house."

"We're on our property."

"No, we aren't." Winnie grinned down at her and pointed a little to her right where their property line butted up against their neighbor's.

"This isn't a joke."

"It's a little bit of a joke."

"Winnie, get *down*." Eliza stomped one foot, hating how childish and out of control she felt. While the Wolf may have been on the other side of the Cape earlier, she didn't know how magic wolves traveled. For all she knew, it could leap across all of Fen in one bound.

Winnie's shoulders slumped. Making as much noise as she could, she pulled herself up so she stood.

An animal howled in the distance. The Wolf. The unearthly sound sank into Eliza's body.

"Hurry," Eliza asked, pinpricks rising along her skin.

Win stood with one hand clasped against the tree's trunk.

"Get down. Now!"

Winnie rose up on her toes, one hand reaching into the open air.

"Winnie!"

She *jumped.*

"No!" Eliza shouted.

Winnie's arms and legs stretched out, as if the wind might catch her, catch *in* her, and push her above the treetops. But instead of soaring up, she fell down. A branch smacked her shoulder, and she screamed.

Adrenaline pumped through Eliza. She ran beneath Winnie. From behind them, Pa and Zilpha shouted and came running. Winnie smacked into Eliza's open arms with a *whump*, and they both tumbled to the ground in a painful heap.

Open and closed, open and closed, Winnie's mouth gaped; she struggled to breathe, but then her lungs inflated, and they did so with a wrenching cry. She gulped in air and let loose terrible tears.

"Winnie. *Winnie.*" Eliza bundled up her sister, ignoring her own bruised body.

"I wanted…" Winnie sucked in a breath, snot running across her face. "I wanted to see the moon."

And then Pa was there, wrapping Winnie in his arms and carrying her toward the house.

Eliza rolled to her knees and stood, one hand pressed against the ache blooming in her hip from where she'd landed. Confusion roiled through her.

One, two, three. Eliza held her breath, pushing all her anxiety into her lungs, and stumbled toward the Jester.

Sixty-six, sixty-seven, sixty-eight. She didn't understand how Dire's bargains worked.

One hundred and one, one hundred and two, one hundred and three. But she knew that Winnie hadn't fallen, she'd jumped, and she'd done so after hearing the Wolf howl. She'd tried to leap for it.

Death by Wolf.

Someone *had* bargained Winnie's life away. Pa would do anything to get Ma back, and now Eliza knew Zilpha missed her mom too, and that she'd bargained before. Maybe one of them had gone to Dire for help, but the only way to get that help was to give up Winnie. One of them had traded Winnie's life for a bargain.

Eliza would find out who, and she'd make them trade it back.

PART II

—

IN WHICH THERE IS A HUNT

TEN

—

Eliza dreamed, though she believed
she dreamed of nothing at all.

I n the middle of the night, wet snuffles at the back door woke
Eliza. She rolled from bed fast enough that the cold of the
floor against her feet and the black of the night against her eyes
confused her senses. She froze.

Two sharp inhales and one long exhale came from the small
crack where the door met the threshold of their home. The Wolf
prowled outside the restaurant.

Eliza tiptoed to the door and rose up to peer out the glass, her sweaty feet leaving prints against the wooden flooring.

Yellow eyes met hers.

Voice wavering, she said, "I don't care what bargain Pa or Zilpha made with your master. You're not allowed to take Winnie." She pressed her nose to the glass, breath smearing condensation around her face and clouding the view of the Wolf on the other side.

The Wolf's mouth parted and its tongue lolled out from between sharp canine teeth. It grunted once, and then turned its monstrous body from the door and trotted into the woods. Eliza watched its progress, fingers curled around the metal fire poker she didn't remember picking up.

She stood guard long after it had disappeared and long after her muscles had started shaking from fatigue.

It was near midnight when she slipped into bed beside Winnie.

~

Eliza couldn't sleep. Some dream caused Winnie's fingers and toes to twitch as she slept, and Eliza turned over, folding her in a hug, trying to chase away any nightmares that might haunt her sister. The knot of hair at the back of her head fluffed in Eliza's face, reminding her of everything she had yet to solve.

Dreams had stuffed Ma's insides thick too, just like Winnie. *They keep me warm against winter's chill*, Ma would say. Which dream had been the one to take Ma away? Winnie was like her, with dreams colliding in the space between her ears, in the chambers of her heart, in the stars of her eyes. But Winnie was little and didn't know better; she didn't know the danger of dreams the same way Eliza did.

Eliza had been careful, *oh* so careful not to dream. She'd been careful to keep Winnie safe. It wasn't enough though, because she hadn't stopped Pa or Zilpha from dreaming up a bargain that was trying to take her sister's life. She knew it had to have been one of them, and she thought she knew what the bargain had been, but *when* had it been made, and how was she supposed to stop it?

She felt on the verge of losing everything—it was this unknowable sense of loss that made her roll over, change clothes, and escape through the front door into the dark.

The Wolf won't kill me. It isn't hunting me. It didn't hurt me on the beach. It wants Winnie, not me. This shaky confidence bolstered her and carried her onto Old Queen Mae.

One, two, three. She skirted around iced-over puddles of water in the road. She kept the collar to her jacket turned down, her warm neck and ears cooling in the night.

Sixty-three, sixty-four, sixty-five. The attack on Winnie

happened before anyone had seen Dire on the Cape, before anyone would've had the chance to make a new bargain—Pa and Zilpha included.

Ninety-four, ninety-five, ninety-six. This meant the bargain that included Winnie must've been made at the end of last winter, before Dire had left for the summer.

One hundred and eleven, one hundred and twelve, one hundred and thirteen. Had it been made earlier, Winnie would've been threatened earlier too.

Eliza knew of one way to search out the truth of this. She exhaled her held breath, bent, snatched up a small stone, and chucked it at a window above the supply shop Mr. Hardwick owned. This wasn't the first time she'd thrown rocks at Filemon's window. It was just the first time she'd done so since she and Filemon had stopped being friends. Not being friends anymore though didn't mean she couldn't ask for favors.

She pinged another, and then another, careless of the fact that if Mr. Hardwick woke, he would call her father who would haul her home.

Filemon's window slid open, and he poked his head through. "Eliza?"

The pebble she'd cradled tumbled to the ground. She held fragile words in her mouth, ones that might break apart the moment she let them lose.

"Eliza?"

"I need help." The words didn't break. They did nothing but hover in the night air. She fidgeted as she waited for Filemon to respond.

"It's the middle of the night. What could you possibly need help with?"

"I'm breaking in someplace."

A grin widened Filemon's mouth. "You should've said that first." He disappeared, sliding shut his window.

Eliza waited in the middle of the street with her arms wrapped around her middle. The still air unnerved her, as if it had eyes, as if something watched from a distance.

Filemon opened his front door. "Where are we breaking into?"

"*I'm* breaking in somewhere. You don't have to come," Eliza said. "So far, nobody's telling me the truth about the Wolf, so I figure I should go to the most reliable source for gossip about bargains on Cape Fen: Mrs. Chess."

"You're breaking into Mrs. Chess's house?"

"No! No." A shudder wracked Eliza's frame; no one had seen odd Mrs. Chess in years. People might talk to her all the time when they picked up their phone and got the telephone operator, but no one had *seen* her. She'd hidden herself away. Eliza didn't want to ask Mrs. Chess questions over the phone where anyone could listen in on the party line, and she sure wasn't brave enough to try and visit Mrs. Chess, but she *was* brave enough to do something else: "I want to break into the library."

What smile had existed on Filemon's face dropped free, sliding to flop against the frozen ground. "I'm not your sidekick, Eliza. I'm not here to do whatever you ask just because you ask it. And it's not breaking in when you have a key. That's what you want, isn't it? You don't want my help—you just want me to give you the key."

"It's the same thing."

"Not really."

Confusion bogged Eliza down.

"I'm not going to *give* you the key. That was my mother's key. I'm not going to just hand it over."

Eliza found she couldn't look away from Filemon's face, though she desperately wanted to. Filemon's mom had died during his birth, and the library had long been run by her side of the family. Eliza used to go with him on the weekends to visit his grandparents.

"I won't lose it," Eliza said, quiet.

"If you're going to the library, I'm going too."

Eliza finally glanced away from him. "All right, fine," she said to the ground. "I just want to read the old newspapers when no one else is around. I don't want anyone to ask me what I'm doing."

Filemon disappeared inside his home, and when he returned, it was with his brother's too-large jacket over his shoulders and one hand fisted in a pocket. "We won't have long. My dad always knows when I'm not close by. I don't want to make him mad by disappearing."

Without hesitation, he turned and led the way. He pulled out a ring of keys from his pocket, and in the middle, a skeleton key as long as Eliza's palm dangled. A pang moved through Eliza, as she watched him squeeze the teeth of the key.

"What's the library got to do with Mrs. Chess?" Filemon asked.

Eliza shook her head. It was one thing to think to herself that her pa or aunt might've bargained away Winnie, but it was another thing entirely to admit it out loud. The idea of it *hurt*.

Filemon didn't ask again when she didn't answer. Instead, they walked in silence for the short trip to the library. The white-bricked building was skinny, though its deceiving depth gave it a monstrous size inside. Metal lettering, painted white, hung on the door, spelling the words *Cape Fen Library* in a dancing script. Beneath it in smaller letters ran the phrase *Dreaming Is to Live*. Filemon fitted the key into the front door's lock and wiggled it, pulling at the old, heavy door. From behind them, wind picked up, rattling the branches of bushes against one another. Eliza watched the flickers of movement as the door creaked open, but the light across the street didn't quite pierce the darkness beyond the shrubbery.

Prickles of unease slid through Eliza. She turned from the darkness and followed Filemon inside, blinking against the change in light as he picked a hand-cranked flashlight off a shelf and wound it up. From there, he led her down the rows of books, their steps echoing against wooden floors and bricked walls.

Pitter-pat, went their steps. *Pitter-pat. Pitter-pat. Pitter—Thump.*

"Filemon?" Eliza whispered, freezing in place, one hand stretched out to grasp his arm.

"*Shh.*" He swung the flashlight behind them, illuminating a figure. Shadows tossed up—hair scattered every which way and a too-long coat billowed as skinny legs tried to run and hide.

Eliza bellowed, "Winnie!"

"*Shh!*" Filemon waved at Eliza. "Keep it down. My grandma will be so mad if she finds us in here. She'll tell Dad, and then he'll never let me out of the house again."

"Winnie, get back here," Eliza whispered harshly.

"I'm a…a ghooost," said Winnie, voice pitched low and gravelly.

"*Winnie!*"

From around a bookshelf, Winnie peeked.

Horrified, Eliza went to her and grabbed her up.

"You're squishing me." Winnie struggled in her grip.

"You're not supposed to be out at night."

"*You're* out at night. You snuck out, so I wanted to sneak out too. You always get to have all the fun."

Eliza pulled away, confused. "I do not! I never have any fun."

"Liza, you're breaking into the library in the middle of the night."

How was she supposed to make Winnie understand that none of this was fun? "This isn't a game, Winnie."

"You're looking for stuff about me," Winnie whispered in her ear.

Eliza pressed her forehead to her sister's. The thick air was swollen, filled up with *watchfulness,* with the quiet need to hurry. "Fine. Yes. Okay. We'll look at the newspapers and then return home. We'll work fast."

Winnie gave a quiet whoop and then wiggled out of Eliza's reach. They trekked across the library by the brilliant light of the almost-full moon shining through wide windows and the yellowing light of Filemon's flashlight. She braced herself, grateful she couldn't truly see the expanse of the library that felt more like a graveyard in the dead of night.

Filemon took them to a door at the back of the library. He

lit a coal-oil lamp that sat on a desk and handed it to them, its gently swaying light throwing dark pictures against their feet. "There's a rope in the middle of the room you can hang this from. Good luck."

"You're not coming with us?"

"I don't like the basement," he said, shuddering, and when Eliza started down, added, "Don't mess anything up. Grandma'll kill me if you ruin anything."

"I won't," Eliza said. She descended the stairs with the lamp in hand, the colder temperatures of the basement cooling the flushed skin of Eliza's bare hands, sending chill bumps over her arms. At the bottom, she found the rope Filemon had mentioned and set the handle of the lamp in a hook tied to the end. The stone room flooded with unnatural, flickering color that tossed moving shadows into every corner.

She'd been in the cool, dry cellar before, but only once when Ma wanted to show her Cape Fen's history. She'd plugged her nose against the musty smell, to which Ma had told her, *It's only the sleeping words of newspapers you're smelling*. Even knowing that, she hadn't much liked the scent.

Wooden crates sat on shelves that lined the basement, and inside those crates were hundreds, if not thousands, of old papers, containing all of the Cape's history. The space didn't feel quite the same without Ma there, but Eliza steeled her nerves and walked into the shadows between the shelves, her steps repeating against the stone floor and walls.

Beside her, Winnie cracked open the lid of a box to find crinkly papers preserved between thin, white cloths. She sneezed, lifting one of the pieces of fabric. Eliza peeled it away and took up the newspaper beneath it, scanning for the gossip column. Mrs. Chess, the columnist, knew everything that happened on Cape Fen, partly because of the phone lines, but also because of a bargain with Dire. No one knew what the bargain had been, though they did know it had resulted in her knowing things she shouldn't have.

Eliza knew she wouldn't find mention of the word *bargain* or mention of Baron Dire in the column, but she also knew there might still be hints of both. She had to at least take a look. She set down the paper she held, closed the box, and moved on, going back in time, while Winnie moved on to another crate. April to March to February—the end of winter when Dire sailed away from the Cape's shore. She popped open the lid and peeled out a paper, being as gentle as she could with the fragile print. She read until her eyes ached, until the tiny letters blurred on the page, until sentences like *Jarvis Bodfish aims to recite the whole of Cape Fen's lore in one sitting* bled into *Lionel Parlett will throw a New Year's bash, complete with candies and champagne shipped in from overseas* combined with *The Sanfords' grocery store will now sell coffee roasted in house.*

Eliza folded her paper and set it in her "read" pile. Mrs. Chess hadn't mentioned Dire and what was worse, she hadn't mentioned Pa or Zilpha either. She asked Winnie, "Have you found anything?"

"No," Winnie said.

Eliza looked over to find her sister sitting cross-legged on top of a box with her hands held in front of her, thumbs hooked together and fingers flying outward, throwing the shadow of a bird onto the wall behind her.

"You're not even reading!" Eliza said.

"I read." Winnie pointed to an open box.

Noticing the date printed on its side, Eliza's heart began to gallop inside her ribs.

She crawled across the floor, rising up on her knees and pressing her palms against the box Winnie pointed to. The lid lay on the ground, and the paper on the top was dated her birthday, four years past.

The date of Ma's leaving.

She thumbed through the pages, flipping to Mrs. Chess's gossip column, frustration mounting as she read about nothing but *parties* and *sailboat competitions* and *the favorite dress-shop of the visiting politicians from the mainland had to put in an extra order for their lace tea dresses for their wives,* and *Sheriff Olavi has been seen hunting for the Wolf since the night of First Frost eight days past, even though, as our lore states, the Wolf cannot be killed.*

But Eliza didn't care about Sheriff Olavi. She cared about Ma. And then...

Tynne Serling was spotted fishing with the Haagertys, preparing for her eldest daughter's birthday. She traded a bottle of her famous sleeping draught for help catching the best fish. Rumor has it that she's interested in visiting family on the continent, though one has to assume she's interested in having family visit her *in the summer. Last week, Doctor Landis assisted in the birth of twins—*

"That's it?" Eliza shoved the paper away from her face. "That's *all* Mrs. Chess writes about Ma? Who cares about Doctor Landis and babies!"

"Babies are cute. They look like potatoes," Winnie said.

"There should be more here! She should've said something else about Ma leaving, not just mention family on the continent."

"Maybe it's in the next week's paper, after Ma disappeared."

But when Eliza checked that paper, all that existed in it was news of the reward money sent in for the fishing competition the Haagertys had won in the middle of summer, and mention of Amelia Bodfish being found by Colby Parlett in the middle of a whiteout fog, and—

"Nothing about Ma," Eliza said.

"Maybe that's not the sort of thing Mrs. Chess writes about."

"It should be." Eliza started packing away the papers, shoving them together hard enough to crinkle their middles. Not only had the papers not mentioned a single thing about Pa or Zilpha from last winter, they hadn't mentioned anything about Ma's leaving. All they had said was that she wanted to visit family.

The waste of the night lay heavy on Eliza. She closed the crate's lid and took Winnie's hand, removing the lantern from the rope and returning to the main floor of the library. They found Filemon sitting on top of a counter, reading a book with his nose close to the spine. When he noticed them, he raised his own lantern up toward the ceiling, where the light passed over swirling dust motes.

"Nice timing. I was about to come get you. My dad'll notice if I'm not back soon." Filemon jumped down and carefully filed his book back on the appropriate shelf. Then, he led the way through the rows of books.

It was as they walked past a shelf with Sir Arthur Conan Doyle's *The Hound of the Baskervilles* that a high whine cut through the hushed night—the front door swinging open.

Winnie stopped and didn't budge when Eliza pushed her onward.

"It's just the door," Eliza said, trying to reassure her sister.

"I *closed* the door," Filemon said.

Winnie took a step back, fear widening her eyes. She whispered, "I didn't."

Eliza's heartbeat thumped against the side of her neck. The watchfulness of the night descended again, pinning the skin between her shoulder blades.

"*Wolf,*" Winnie said, pointing behind them.

Eliza turned to look.

By the moonlight that shone through one of the long library windows, the Wolf's gray coat bleached to white. It sat beside the counter Filemon had read on with its tail swishing against the ground, sweeping away any footprints Eliza and Winnie might've left behind.

Beside her, Winnie took a step forward with hands outstretched. Eliza lurched toward her, blocking her path.

"*Run fast,*" she hissed, shoving Winnie toward the front door.

"Eliza?" Filemon asked, but Eliza was already running, pushing Winnie before her, fear thrumming through her muscles and expanding her senses.

Adrenaline slowed the moment: the crunch of feet against the ground, the wheeze of air through tightened throats, the flicker of Winnie's hair before her, the swoosh of her inner arms against sleeves, the beat of the Wolf's paws as it raced behind.

Winnie hesitated at the threshold of the open door, and

Eliza pushed her through. Winnie raced forward, running down the stairs and tripping down the last two.

"*Winnie!*" The shout wrenched from Eliza's throat as she scrambled after, snatching Win up by the armpits. She half carried her down the street, Filemon taking Winnie's other arm. She didn't dare look behind. Time darted from her grasp, flying loose as she searched for a hiding spot. A tree to climb. A house to escape into. A car to leap on top of.

"Faster!" Eliza cried.

The Wolf's howl started up. Without looking, she knew it hovered at the top of the library stairs.

"Wolves can't climb trees!" Eliza shouted. She grabbed Winnie and shoved her toward a tree, boosting her up to a low-hanging branch. She shoved at her feet, helping her onto the limb, and looked to find Filemon climbing the tree beside theirs, shimmying up faster even than Winnie, who was as at home among the trees as a bird.

"Climb, climb!" Winnie screamed down at her.

The patter of sharp nails on stone steps came from the direction of the library. The thump of paws on pavement. The whoosh of the Wolf cutting through the night—Eliza jumped. Missed. Jumped. *Missed.* She jumped and tried to grab at the branch, not quite able to catch hold of its thickness without someone pushing her up from behind.

"Liza!" Winnie screamed.

Eliza turned and raced toward Filemon's tree. The branch there was skinnier, and her hands wrapped around it with ease. Feet scrabbling against the trunk, she hauled herself up, and with Filemon's help, she climbed onto the branch and then onto the one above it. Eliza turned, holding tight to a thin twig to keep her balance. Was Winnie high enough? How far had she climbed?

The Wolf appeared between their trees, nose lifting and huffing at the air. It faced Winnie's tree, and with one smooth motion, stretched itself up.

The Wolf rose higher and higher, paws scratching at the bark and reaching toward Winnie's toes. Winnie whimpered and tucked herself closer to the trunk, scooting her feet as far out of the Wolf's range as she could. The Wolf growled, sound slipping between its sharp teeth.

Eliza twisted the twig she held, desperately breaking and re-breaking it, trying to snap the green wood from the trunk. She burst out, "Filemon, please. Help," and wrenched at the twig, ripping it free. She turned and hurled it at the Wolf, screaming, "Leave her *alone!*"

The branch fell on the Wolf, landing on its head and doing no damage, but all the same, the Wolf dropped back onto its haunches. It glanced at her, eyes glowing bright with moonlight, then it leaned back, muscles bunching, preparing to leap—

"Higher, Winnie. *Climb higher!*" Eliza scooted toward the end of her branch, her feet slipping on the wood. Filemon grabbed the back of her jacket and saved her from falling to the earth.

The Wolf howled, a snarling mess of a sound.

A gunshot cleaved the Wolf's howl in two. Scared witless, Eliza wrapped her arms and legs around the tree trunk. The Wolf cowered at the base of Winnie's tree, frozen at the unbearably loud noise of the gun.

"Wolf!" a voice called out.

One, two, three…

"I've been hunting for you." *Sheriff Olavi!*

Seven, eight, nine…

"Stay still, and let me put you in the ground once and for all."

Twelve, thirteen, fourteen…

Sheriff Olavi stood down the street with her rifle pointed at the Wolf.

"I told you to keep away last winter," Sheriff Olavi shouted, "but you couldn't leave well enough alone. You had to come back. You had to keep haunting this place. Why can't you just leave us alone?"

Eliza didn't know who to be more afraid of: the sheriff with the gun or the Wolf with the claws.

"*Why can't you leave us alone?*" Sheriff Olavi raised the rifle to her shoulder.

One, two, three. Eliza covered her head, prayed that Sheriff Olavi wouldn't aim too high.

The shot blasted the air. Her ears filled with a strange, high-pitched ring that drowned out the other sounds of the night. Eliza trembled with palms pressed to her ears. Footsteps and panting breaths and a muffled, growling yelp exploded along the street. A third shot came, and Eliza watched as the Wolf turned and ran, escaping down the street. Sheriff Olavi shouted. She ran too, crossing the road and heading after the Wolf.

Silence descended, broken only by the harsh breaths Eliza couldn't contain. Her arms shook as she slid off the branch and fell to the ground. Stumbling to her feet, she stretched her hands toward Winne. Win reached out her arms, too, and fell off her branch, tumbling straight into Eliza. Twice in one night, Eliza had caught her sister as she'd fallen like a baby bird unable to fly. They both dropped into a heap on the ground. Winnie quivered, her face hidden against Eliza's shoulder.

Eliza said to Filemon, "Sheriff Olavi might come back, and I...I—"

"I don't want to see her, either," Filemon said, as he joined them. "I don't think she saw us. Let's keep it that way."

From far away, a car door slammed.

"Is she back?" Filemon asked.

"Shh," Eliza said, fear shoving exhaustion through her limbs. "*Shh*."

Footsteps crunched against the road, the gravel talking as if giving up secrets. *Someone's coming,* it said. They came closer, footsteps certain in the cold night. But then the footsteps stopped, because they weren't near the tree but *beside* the tree. A face peered around the trunk, and an involuntary shuddering breath left Eliza.

"You planning on sleeping here?" Zilpha leaned against the trunk.

Relief swamped Eliza. Sobs hiccupped from her belly. It took a moment for the tears to come, but when they did, they left hot tracks down her cheeks. She didn't question how Zilpha had come to be there. She merely accepted it, because it meant someone would keep them safe.

From beside Eliza, Winnie said, "I want to go home."

And without comment, Zilpha reached down, scooped up Winnie, and pulled Eliza and Filemon along with her.

ELEVEN

—

Waylon Serling dreamed. He plugged his ears and
hummed a tune, praying Baron Dire wouldn't hear.

Zilpha returned them to the Jester with a firm command to *sleep*. Exhausted, but unable to for the jitters adrenaline had left in its wake, Eliza lay on her cot and remembered the incident at the library over and over, replaying the details of Winnie stuck in the tree and Eliza unable to do a single thing to help. She knew that without Sheriff Olavi, the Wolf would've found a way to climb the tree and gobble up her sister. Twice now, they'd been lucky. If the Wolf came a third time, they couldn't trust their luck to hold.

Sweat rolled down her temples. It soaked the backside of her ears and slicked down her inner arms. Uncomfortable, she kicked off her covers and mashed her eyes shut. Behind her lids, fuzzy shapes formed, drifting along on wavelike patterns. The world tipped a bit, rocking as if she lay on a boat. She turned over and the world righted itself, only to slip back loose again a moment later. There seemed to be two parts of herself: one solid as ever and the other trying to slide free.

In a rush of frustration, she rolled off her bed. Keeping herself busy, she worked through her chore schedule for the day. She cooked oatmeal and set it outside to cool, cleaned the ash from the potbelly stove, darned a hole in Winnie's sock, and dusted Ma's stained glass lamp. Looking through the yellow stars, she thought about the newspaper. *Rumor has it that she's interested in visiting family on the continent,* it had said. *Though one has to assume she's interested in having family visit* her *in the summer.*

Maybe Eliza had learned something at the library after all. What if the first part was true? What if Ma had gone off the Cape to live with family on the continent? If that's what Ma had bargained for, what had she bargained away to get off the Cape? Worse, what if Eliza had been wrong all along and it was neither Pa nor Zilpha who'd bargained away Winnie's life?

Eliza had assumed that since Ma left four years ago that her bargain would have nothing to do with the bargain made against Winnie. But her assumption could be as wrong as the assumption the newspaper had made.

Truly, Pa, Zilpha, *or* Ma could've been the one to bargain away her sister.

A plan knit itself tight inside her; she needed to understand more about her mother and more about Dire's magic.

The sun rose. Eliza got ready, and when she deemed the world awake—perhaps not quite awake *enough* but as awake as she could stand—she sat on the edge of her sister's cot and smoothed her hands over Winnie's head, patting down the tangle of knots at the back of her willowy-white hair. Pulling the covers over Winnie's shoulders, she was surprised to find a small feather tucked beneath the pillow.

Winnie blinked blearily at her, then smiled at the plume. "I dreamed of flying." She clutched her owl. One of its wooden wings peeked from beneath the covers.

"You shouldn't pick feathers up from outside." Eliza stood and placed the feather in the stove. "I'm going on an errand. Breakfast's on the table. I'll be back soon."

With that, she kissed Win on the forehead and grabbed a light coat before leaving the Jester. She was hot and didn't bother buttoning the front as she headed into the thick morning fog and toward the one person who might know the answers she so desperately needed.

Soon enough, she stood before the Chess house, eyeing each of the darkened windows much the same way she often eyed the darkened ocean, wondering what hid behind the curtain at the surface. The window shades didn't flicker or move, and they weren't twitched aside by a hand to reveal the face of a woman no one had seen in years.

Eliza knocked hard on the door. No answer. She knocked again, pounding the side of her fist against the wooden slab, and when that didn't work, she kicked the toe of her boot into the base. No answer still.

"I know you're in there! I need to talk with you. *Please.*" Humiliation washed through her at the last word. *Please.* It sounded so sad, so weak. "*Please, please, please,*" she whispered with her forehead pressed to the door; she would say it a hundred times more if it meant keeping Winnie safe.

"What're you doing?"

Eliza whirled. Filemon stood behind her, fog misting off his shoulders and curling his hair, a sketchpad in one hand and pencil in the other—a second chunk of lead rested behind one ear. "I think I found a clue in the newspapers last night, but I need to know more. I want to talk to Mrs. Chess."

"I could help more, you know." Filemon shaded a line on

the page of his sketchpad. "If you want to talk to me about what you found."

Eliza folded her arms, clasping her elbows tight, not knowing what to make of Filemon. The darkness of the night before had made it easier to talk to him, when she couldn't see the circles beneath his eyes or the way his cheekbones cut into his skin, as if he weren't eating enough. He looked sad and confused inside his brother's bulky coat.

Are you all right? she thought to ask, but the question made her uncomfortable, and so she said, "I'm going to try and talk with Mrs. Chess."

Eliza turned back toward the door and knocked again.

"Good luck, Eliza. I hope she answers," Filemon said and shuffled away, dragging with him the feeling that she should've asked for something or should've accepted his help. But what would he have done? Helped her knock on the Chesses' door?

She knocked again, but just as she did, the knob clicked, bolts to the lock falling out of place, and the door cracked open. With her weight pressed into it, she stumbled. She caught herself with one hand on the frame and the other on the knob, and her feet tread onto thin carpet that masked the sound of her steps.

"Mrs. Chess?" she called into the darkened foyer. She moved forward and let the door swing closed behind her, shutting out the wet tang of mist and the fragile sunlight that tried to break through.

But for a steady coal-oil lamp sitting on a side table, no lights shimmered inside the Chess home. She picked up the lamp by its handle and was careful to hold it out of her sight line so as not to blind herself. She passed through the front foyer and headed down an unlit hall, footsteps muffled by the carpet. Pausing, she bent and ran her fingers over the soft flooring. She'd never been in a house with carpet before, and as she petted it, a closed-up, musty smell was released, as if the house hadn't been opened to outside air in years.

"Mrs. Chess?" Eliza stood and took a step. The flame in her hand flickered and sent shadows dancing at the edges of her vision. Her breath pulled tight in her chest and skin prickled with scare-bumps. She cleared her throat and wished now for Filemon, if only to have him nearby for comfort. "Mrs. Chess?"

"Is the light enough?" Mrs. Chess asked, voice raspy. She sounded as if she had a terrible cold.

Holding the lantern high to cast light in a wider circle about her, Eliza turned in the direction of the woman's voice. She faced the opening to a room. "The light's enough. I haven't tripped over anything."

"I find myself not needing light like I used to, and my husband kindly agrees to keep the electric lights off. It saves on the power bill, anyway, which he likes plenty." Mrs. Chess's voice originated from a pool of darkness in one corner of the room.

"You know what everyone's bargained," Eliza blurted. "I want to know about them, about the bargains."

"Isn't that what we all want to know? I certainly do. In fact, it's all I've ever dreamed of."

"Please. Tell me about them, tell me a—abou…" Eliza's voice tried to dart away from her, but she held it fast and managed to spit out, "Tell me what my mother bargained."

"How very direct of you."

"I don't have time to waste."

"Not even for a quick hello? A 'How are you, Mrs. Chess? So very nice of you to let me in.'"

Eliza's cheeks flushed with shame. "I'm sorry. I didn't think. That was rude of me." She stepped inside and reached out to brace herself against the wall to her right. Soft warmth met her skin, and she pulled back with a gasp.

"Nothing but cloth," Mrs. Chess said.

Eliza reached out again and slid her hands over the lengths of thick, textured fabric that hung over the wall. By the warmth and dampened sounds in the room, she knew it covered every wall. She tried to make Mrs. Chess happy, saying, "Hello. How are you, Mrs. Chess? It's very nice of you to let me in your home."

"*Psh.* Leave niceties aside, now. The damage is already done. And stay where you are. My eyes can't take the light."

Eliza paused where she stood. She wanted to see the extent of the cloth-wrapped room and the place where the darkness hung thickest about Mrs. Chess's shoulders, but something held her back.

"Tell me what you want to know about bargains."

In a rush, Eliza said, "I thought either Pa or Aunt Zilpha might've bargained away Winnie to get Ma back, but I read in one of your old newspapers that my ma wanted to visit family on the continent. It's not possible to *visit* family on the continent. So I thought, maybe my ma did it... Maybe she bargained away Winnie to be able to leave the Cape. I need to know what happened."

Mrs. Chess laughed. "You don't. Not really. All you *need* to know is how to break whatever bargain exists against your sister."

"So there *is* a bargain against her! I knew it!"

Mrs. Chess moved where she sat, the heavy folds of darkness around her shifting at her shoulders. "It's too bad that there isn't a way to *break* bargains. Once a bargain is struck, there's no real way to change it, since Dire refuses to use his magic to undo what's already been done."

"Then why did you tell me that to begin with? You got my hopes up."

"To make sure that you know you're not the first person

who's tried to understand Dire's magic. Not many know how his bargains work, Eliza; I merely listen for what people *have* bargained. If you want to understand how they work, you have to go to the Parletts."

Everything inside Eliza clammed up, sweat from her palm slicking the wire handle of the lamp. No part of her wanted to go to the Parletts, where Loretta grieved Kendare, and where Lionel and her cousins traded in Dire's magic the same way some traded in bread and honey and cheese for washing chores in the middle of summer. Like it was easy. Like it didn't matter. Like it didn't steal away family members. "Please tell me more about my ma's bargain. Did she give up my sister so she could get off the Cape?"

"That's where you're going wrong, Eliza."

"She made a bargain. It's the only way she could've disappeared. She left us!"

"She left you, and while that's very sad, there isn't anything in Dire's rules that says bargains must always be for the better. If a man wishes for the ability to breathe water and they give up their ability to breathe air, have things really gotten better?"

"N-no."

"If a woman asks for protection and is granted the ability to put a grown man to sleep with the touch of a hand, but loses all ability to touch anyone, are they happier?"

"I—yes?"

"If someone bargains to escape a life they believe they loathe even though they must cut ties to their family to do so, are they better off than they were to begin with?"

"Not unless they hate their family."

"Bargains appear to be equal when people feel stuck, but they rarely are when they're lived out, and they're *not* usually for the better."

Eliza shook her head, trying to rid it of the cobwebs Mrs. Chess had spun there. "That doesn't help. That doesn't tell me about the attack against Winnie or about Ma's leaving. The Wolf made to eat Winnie, but I pushed her out of the way. It came for her again last night! The Wolf only goes after those who've tried to escape a bargain or those who've run out of time or those who've bargained their life away."

Though she couldn't see her, Eliza swore Mrs. Chess was grinning from across the room.

"The Wolf is only a servant of Dire's," Mrs. Chess said. "It doesn't kill outright, Eliza. Just look at what happened with Kendare."

"Doctor Landis said Kendare drowned, but that's a lie."

"It's not a lie. Kendare drowned, he just drowned in air." Mrs. Chess sighed. She leaned forward. "Forget Pa. Forget Zilpha. Neither of them would bargain away your sister, and shame on you for thinking it."

Eliza flushed, but she refused to feel bad. She would think whatever she needed to save Winnie. "Then it was Ma who bargained away Winnie's life."

"Bargained *for*, Eliza. You're going wrong again."

"Ma bargained for Winnie's life? But how do you bargain *for* and what does that mean?"

The edges of Eliza's light touched the place where Mrs. Chess's feet met the floor and where her toes tapped with impatience.

From somewhere in the house, a door clicked open. "Ladi?" called Mr. Chess. His footsteps thumped as he walked through the stuffy, closed-up home.

"Time for you to go," Mrs. Chess said.

"No, not before you tell me," said Eliza.

"No more hints, girl. I've already given you more than you deserve. Perhaps you should've been kinder when you entered."

"You've confused me, all because I didn't say a proper hello? My sister could die." Eliza took two vicious steps forward and thrust the light above her head. "It's not fair! It's not—"

Mrs. Chess snarled. Her eyes slammed shut and arms shot up to block the light. From between the fluffy hair on her head, two leathery ears stuck out from the top of her skull. Ears covered the side of her scalp, the back of it, the top. Bat ears and canine ears and rabbit ears. Eliza screamed and dropped the lantern. The light plunged out. She spun and barreled through the doorway, smacking into Mr. Chess's squishy chest.

"What—"

Eliza shoved Mr. Chess as hard as she could. He staggered, and she darted by, tripping over her feet and landing on her knees. She scrambled for the end of the hall, wrenched open the door, and plunged into the haze that covered Old Queen Mae.

TWELVE

Mrs. Chess dreamed. Bat ears perked up, she listened to the whispers someone spoke while they slumbered, all the consonants softened by sleep and vowels strung together by open-mouthed inhalations. She jotted notes onto a pad of paper. What good gossip it all would make come morning.

Eliza meant to head for home, but her feet were too scared, and her mind was too shattered, and she ran before she could make sense of the direction she took. Filemon shouted behind her, but her body kept moving. Trees loomed out of the mist and smacked at her cheeks. She raised her arms to protect her face and ran harder, through the woods and down the path where she'd seen the Wolf. Adrenaline fuzzed the thoughts that commanded her to *stop, focus, think.* She ran and ran, her boots thumping against mud, then dune grass, then beaded rocks and sand, until at last she tromped into Fen Bay.

She dropped to her knees, dry heaving, and shoved her hands into the water. The shock of cold jolted her, and she looked up and across the white-tipped ocean. *Chop-chop, chop-chop,* went the waves as they strode up the beach and drenched her skirts. It soothed her. Her fingers warmed against the cold of the water. The tireless ocean quieted her racing mind, washing away the confusion of animal ears on a human head, and—

One, two, three. The ocean slicked over her skin, and she stopped thinking.

Eighty-eight, eighty-nine, ninety. She leaned forward, wishing, hoping, dreaming for the safety of the water. She fell toward the waves.

One hundred and sixty-three, one hundred and sixty-four, one hundred and sixty-five. The ocean caught her. The bay closed over her head. She languished in the liquid, arms spread wide, gray coat dragging her toward the bottom.

Her skin, inches thick, protected her from the winter freeze.

Warmth cocooned her and spread out from her core, heating even the very tips of her toes.

The waves gently flipped her over. Eyes open, peering up at the sun through a layer of water, she expected to see mist and clouds and the frail light of morning, but instead, Filemon's hands reached out for her, burning hot and real.

~

Eliza woke to the heat of a fire against her cheeks. "Winnie?" she murmured. She cracked open her eyes, and the blurred image of a white-painted potbelly stove greeted her. The last time she was in Filemon's house, she'd stood awkwardly behind Pa while he borrowed tools from Basil Hardwick, trying not to meet Filemon's eye.

"I found you half-drowned on the beach," Filemon said, his voice tinny and distant.

A shudder wracked her frame. She'd been panicked, and her body had run to the safest place it could think of—the ocean. She clutched blankets over her shoulders and pushed away the hot water bottle that had been set against her torso. On the inside, she didn't feel cold, but when she touched the skin on her nose, her arms, her tummy, it was chilly and clammy, and she was more confused than ever.

"Mrs. Chess." Her throat tightened, and she was unable to

say the words *bat ears*. She sank into the comfort of the soft bedding, pulling it tight around her shoulders to push away the terrifying image.

Filemon appeared in front of her, grinning and holding a mug that read, *Cape Fen, Where Reality Becomes a Dream*. From it swirled the telltale scent of the cranberries the Bodfishes harvested. Filemon held out the tea, and Eliza greedily took it up. Winding her fingers around the warmth and placing her face over the steam, she inhaled, but then had to turn away. The heat of it was too much, and she longed for the cold of the ocean.

She asked, "How did I get here?"

"I did the fireman carry," Filemon said, "and the beach isn't too far away."

She set the mug on the table beside her.

"You've been sleeping for hours and hours. Dad wanted to let you rest longer, but we need to get you home soon. Mrs. Gorham called and said a big storm will land soon. You know she's never wrong. Dad called your pa, so he knows you're here."

Eliza shrank into the covers. What was she supposed to tell Pa? *I decided to go swimming with my shoes and coat on and couldn't stay above the water. Sorry.* Or, should she tell the truth? *I saw Mrs. Chess's head and got so confused, I ran into the ocean and didn't want to get back out.* She had the feeling he wouldn't like either answer.

Filemon crouched beside the couch. Pencil lead covered his nose and cheek, where he'd likely swiped his fingers while drawing. He said, "Why'd you go into the water?"

"Why do you want to help me so much?" Of all the things to ask, this was the question that popped free.

Filemon turned away, putting his back to the couch and sitting on the floor. "We used to help each other all the time. Why's it a big deal?"

"We stopped being friends a long time ago."

"No, *you* stopped being friends with *me*. I was always your friend."

Eliza stopped herself from curling deeper into the couch, and said, "My ma left. I didn't have time for friends."

"My mom's always been gone." Filemon thumbed the corner of a page in his sketchpad. "It's always just been me, Dad, and Bri, but then Bri left, and so now it's just me and Dad. Who do you think does all the cooking and chore work? Me. I do everything, and I do it with Dad watching my every move. He doesn't let me go anywhere. Ever."

"None of us can go anywhere."

"I don't mean off the Cape. I mean anywhere by myself. I've got cabin fever. My dad checks on me throughout the night. He walks me to school. He always knows where I am. He told me he bargained for it—he has magic to keep track of me. He's so scared I'm going to leave like Bri did. He keeps saying he wouldn't survive me leaving and him being alone. All I want is somebody to talk about it with. I need a friend."

"I need a friend too," Eliza whispered. Hearing Filemon's story released something in her, and she said, "I'm sorry I stopped being friends. I just hurt so bad all the time. It never goes away."

"I didn't know my mom, but I still miss her all the time. That never goes away either." Filemon met her gaze. "Will you tell me why you ran from Mrs. Chess's house?"

Unexpected tears came to her eyes. They slipped down her cheeks and into her mouth as salty as the ocean.

"Oh…okay. Okay. Please don't cry."

She didn't swipe away her tears, not caring that she was indeed crying and he was indeed watching. Their friendship couldn't possibly become more awkward than what it was already. The truth gummed up her insides, and she worked to pry it free. Choosing to trust Filemon took more work than she would've imagined, but she'd been telling the truth: she needed a friend.

She said, "Someone bargained with Baron Dire and placed Winnie as the price. That's why the Wolf attacked. I thought it was Pa or Zilpha trying to get Ma back, but Mrs. Chess said not to worry about either of them. She said it was Ma. So that means Ma bargained to get off the Cape, like your brother did, not that I know what Bri bargained—"

"I do." Filemon lifted his arms in a *how do I explain this* gesture. "It's not all that interesting, really. Dad said Bri and Miss Alayna fell in love slow, whatever that means. She used to visit Fen every summer with her family. She and Bri got to know one another years ago. Somehow, Bri convinced her to swap places with him. She stayed past First Frost, and then he left."

"Baron Dire doesn't let people swap places."

"He does when they're pregnant. Two for one. Dire lost Bri but got Miss Alayna and a baby."

Unexpected shock stopped Eliza short. "Bri tricked her?"

"I don't know that he tricked her, really. I think Miss Alayna knew what she was doing when she entered into the swap. Maybe she just didn't realize that Bri wouldn't come back once he left Fen. My dad's still torn up about it. Bri calls sometimes, but Dad doesn't often agree to talk. Most of the time he hangs up the telephone without really answering."

"I'm sorry," she said. "I didn't know." The strangest part of hearing this story was that Filemon knew exactly how his brother had managed to leave Cape Fen, when Eliza didn't know her mother's bargain at all. There was trust between the Hardwicks. They'd shared all their secrets, each of them knowing the bargains the others had struck. It was the clear opposite of the Serlings.

"Why would you have known? So much weird stuff happens

here, it's like none of it really matters." He pushed hair out of his eyes. "Have you considered that Winnie might've made a bargain of her own? We can bargain too. Age doesn't much matter. I mean, look at the Parletts."

Eliza squirmed away from thoughts about Ma's family. *Meeting Dire and his Wolf is a rite of passage,* Colby had said. "I already asked Winnie if she bargained. Besides, she would never."

"She might've."

"She never—"

"But it's possible—"

"No!"

Filemon reached out and patted Eliza on the knee. "Did Mrs. Chess say anything else helpful?"

"Just that Ma probably didn't bargain *away* Winnie, but bargained *for* her instead, but I don't understand that."

Footsteps came from down the hall, from the front where the Hardwicks kept their shop. "That'll be Dad coming to take you home. But…Eliza? I'll help. You know I'll help. You can trust me."

"I believe you." She smiled feebly, liking how this sort of friendship felt inside her. The *trust* shape of it didn't take up space, but rather *gave* her space. Gave her the space to breathe.

THIRTEEN

—

Bri Hardwick dreamed, but he lived on
the continent and was now too far away
for Baron Dire's magic to reach.

Mr. Hardwick walked Eliza to the Fen Jester, saying, "Going to be a bad one, isn't it?" when storm winds whipped up and dragged Eliza's still-drying hair around her head.

She walked beside him, knowing full well that while he certainly wasn't the first adult she'd ever been around who'd bargained, he was the first she'd known about. He was the same person he'd been before, but he felt different now to her, as if he'd changed. Really though, she supposed she'd been the one to change. It made her feel worse about abandoning Filemon too. She supposed that's what happened to friendship though. It grew and altered over time, and that had to be okay.

Mr. Hardwick left her at the door of the Jester, then turned right back around to head home.

Eliza didn't see Pa inside and went to check on Winnie, who sat on her cot playing with her owl, which she'd tied to a string and swung back and forth in the air as if it were flying.

"You drowned?" Win asked, stress showing in the sallowness of her cheeks.

"No, I didn't." Forcing out a lie, she said, "I slipped and fell in the water, and Filemon pulled me out."

Winnie squinted. "That's it?"

"That's it."

The back door opened, and Pa walked through. He stopped when he saw her and folded his arms.

Eliza folded hers as well.

Peering down at her, he asked, "Swimming at the start of winter, Eliza?"

"I tripped and fell. The ocean pulled me in." She dug her fingers into her forearms to brace herself, thinking again on how the Hardwicks didn't lie to each other as she was doing right now to her pa.

"That's not like you."

"The rocks were slippery."

"It's a beach by the ocean," Winnie said. "The rocks are always slippery."

"Exactly my point," Eliza said.

"You've never slipped before." Winnie folded her arms too. The Serlings were a matching trio, arms crossed over chests as if the stance could protect against each other's anger.

"Either way, you weren't being safe. Be safe." Pa's arms unfolded. Winnie's did too. Eliza's did not.

Pa returned to the front of the Jester then to lock the front door and make sure the windows were shuttered. Eliza was left with relief tingling in her fingertips, even as the furious thought *that's it?* slithered through her. Of course that was it—Pa wouldn't give her more than a warning to "be safe." It was Eliza's job to care for herself any more than that.

Were it not for Filemon, she'd probably be dead in the water. Why did Pa not care?

She slammed her fists against her thighs. The hard pain of it thumped through her, echoing what she felt on the inside.

"Eliza?" Winnie whimpered.

She worked free her fingers from where they'd turned into hammers. "I'm just angry, is all."

"I love you," Winnie said, her worry evident by the wrinkle between her brows.

"I love you too." Eliza wrapped Winnie in a hug, willing the upset to seep from her pores into the drafty Fen Jester air and not touch her sister.

The storm Mrs. Gorham had predicted landed not an hour later, complete with torrential, sideways rain and gusts of wind that sent the Jester into fits of creaks and groans.

Winnie huddled beneath the bar and played with her owl, her eyes wide as saucers and her hair sticking straight up in the back from where she'd nervously rubbed her head until it was bright with static. She startled every time the wind rattled the windows.

Bang, bang, bang! Someone pounded on the Jester's front door.

"Who'd be out in this mess?" Pa asked and threw wide the door.

The top of the door frame arched high overhead, but still, Mr. Chess ducked his head when he entered. Eliza sidled up next to the counter, wishing she could hide beneath it like Winnie.

Mr. Chess slid off his sodden coat and let it land in a heap on the floor, waving to Pa not to bother with hanging it up. He said, "It's soaked all the way through anyway."

"At least let me place it by the stove," Pa said. "You'll want something semidry to wear whenever you head back home, though I'm not letting you go until the storm settles."

"Whatever you'd like." Mr. Chess's gaze swept over the Jester until it landed on Eliza.

She froze with arms held stiff by her sides, unsure what she was supposed to say.

"Hello," Winnie said in a quiet voice, which jogged Eliza's mind and she said hello too.

Mr. Chess nodded and sat at the bar. "It's a bad storm and a bad night. I couldn't stay at home."

An uncontrollable tremble arched up Eliza's back as she thought of Mrs. Chess and her head of animal ears back at the Chess house. She took plates off the shelves beneath the bar and set them along the counter, taking care to arrange the silverware exactly how her ma had taught her years ago. Mr. Chess might confuse her, but he still deserved a proper place setting.

"I'm sorry for interrupting your night," Mr. Chess said.

"You're fine, Chess," Pa said. "The casserole should be near to finished."

Eliza pulled the winter mishmash from the gas cook stove, set it on a hot plate on the bar, and stuck a ladle in the middle. Stooping beneath the lip of the bar, she crouched beside her sister. Winnie's eyes stared up at her, pupils disappearing into the black outer ring. Fear radiated off her in a tangible wave, sharp and pungent.

Eliza rubbed her knuckles against Winnie's cheek.

"I don't like the storm," Winnie said.

"You never like storms. You'll be okay."

"I found a feather. Two feathers," Winnie whispered. She held up her owl, showing where she'd tied them to its back.

"*Winnie*, I told you not to pick them up."

"I'm trying not to."

"Where do you keep getting them?"

"My hair!"

"Well stop standing below nests in the woods. This is what happens when you play in the trees." Eliza combed through Winnie's hair. "No more. You're feather-free," she declared to her sister, not including the fact that the big knot of hair at the back of her head had grown.

Winnie's terrified gaze didn't calm. Light flashed outside the Jester with thunder following. The crash shook the windows and set Eliza on edge as well.

"It's just lightning and thunder, Win," she said.

Winnie cradled her owl. "It's just that you can't fly in storms. I don't like it."

"Then it's a good thing you have feet to walk on and a house to sleep in."

"What if all the rain gets in my dreams, and I can't fly?"

Eliza took the owl from Winnie and replaced it with a plate of casserole. "If water gets in your dreams, you'll have to swim. Be a seal instead of a raven."

Winnie cast a stricken glance at the wooden owl that Eliza had set on the floor. "I would never be a raven."

"Eat your food, Win." Eliza stood to find both Pa and Mr. Chess inhaling the dinner concoction of cod and quartered potatoes and vegetables baked just right.

Mr. Chess finished his meal fast enough and pushed away his plate. He folded his hands, lacing his fingers in one direction and then the next, repeating the motion again and again.

"Is there something else I can help you with?" Pa asked. "I'm assuming you didn't only come for dinner."

Mr. Chess's gaze skittered from Pa to land on Eliza, only to dart away again, and she got the feeling the man had come to speak to her more than he had to Pa. She leaned over her food and ate carefully, showing Mr. Chess that she was listening, even if he didn't want to talk directly to her.

"When I…" He folded, unfolded, refolded his hands. "My memory isn't what it was."

"Start at the beginning, Chess," Pa said.

"Yes, right. The beginning. Long ago when Ladi—"

Mrs. Chess.

"—was first imagining what bargain she could ask for, she debated it endlessly. What she wanted most was to hear things. To know the bargains people wanted to make when they were just whispers they spoke to themselves in the middle of the night.

She decided on it and made her bargain with Dire. Because of it, she was changed. She got what she wanted, but it wasn't how she'd pictured it. His magic never quite goes how anyone thinks it will. Ladi says it's because he's rather bad at his magic, but I don't know about that."

Eliza filed this away. Bargaining with a witch who wasn't any good at their craft didn't seem like a good idea. Why would anyone do it?

"Ladi was miserable, and because I loved her, I was miserable too. Ladi went back to him to try and have it undone, but he refused. In the end, I went to Dire to make a bargain of my own to try to fix what had happened to Ladi, or at least to make it better. I bargained for her, but this was my mistake: I didn't plan enough. Ladi had planned for years, and it still went wrong, so I didn't plan at all." Mr. Chess's eyes roved back and forth, as if he was watching the past unfold in front of him. "I didn't know what Dire would want, so I offered every bargain I could think of: a beat of my heart, my most prized memory, my favorite pair of boots, the press of grass under my feet during summer, shades of red," Mr. Chess continued, rambling on and on, words tumbling from his mouth, bargains and hopes piling one on top of the other.

Eliza struggled to keep up.

"I didn't know how the bargains worked, and I didn't

know what Dire would want. I didn't know that he would want anything at all." Mr. Chess focused his gaze on Eliza. Then: "Dire asked for a year of my life."

"You agreed?" Pa asked.

"Of course," Mr. Chess said.

"And he took that year?"

"I don't...I don't really know."

From beneath the counter, Winnie asked, "Was Mrs. Chess okay?"

"Ladi was...better." Mr. Chess's eyes fluttered closed.

What had Mrs. Chess's bargain looked like to begin with, then, if bat ears and rabbit ears were...better?

"I'm not sure I understand why you're telling us this," Pa said.

"Sometimes I wish I could remember where my year disappeared to. Sometimes I wish I knew where I'd gone. You know, they gave me a gravestone? I was eight months disappeared, and Sheriff Olavi ruled me dead and gone. I wasn't dead, I was just gone."

Eliza remembered this—Mrs. Chess had refused to be present for the memorial when Sheriff Olavi fitted the gravestone in place. Cape Fen gossiped on it, just as they gossiped on everything.

"Other times I'm sure I don't want to remember, that

remembering would hurt me more than forgetting, but I—I'm sorry. Really, I came to ask if I could take a bottle of your sleeping draught home for Ladi. She's had trouble sleeping. We both have had trouble sleeping since we bargained." Mr. Chess slumped on his stool, the bump in his spine curving into the shape of a harsh question mark.

"You know I do my best to help," Pa said and rose, heading to the back kitchen where he kept small bottles of the sleeping draught Eliza's ma had made and that Pa had become obsessed with creating.

Eliza's heart sunk. The people Pa did his best to help were always other people, never his daughters. She couldn't very well complain about it though, not while Mr. Chess sat in front of her with his heart split apart.

Mr. Chess gave her a sad smile. "Sometimes I think the tonic your family makes is magic. It makes us sleep dreamless at night."

Pa set the bottle on the countertop.

Mr. Chess took it between shaking hands and cradled it to his chest. "Thank you." He made to leave the Jester, but Pa insisted the man stay, saying, "You were fool enough to travel in this weather. I'll not be the one knocking on Ladi's door come morning with the news that I let you from my house during torrential rains to drown in the middle of Old Queen Mae."

Eliza dragged a stiff mattress down the stairs and made up a bed for Mr. Chess on the floor where the house was warm and not half-frozen like the second floor.

Winnie crawled out from under the counter and onto Eliza's cot. She looked at Mr. Chess and said, "I hope you sleep good. I dream of flying."

"I hope I don't dream. There are always wolves there," Mr. Chess said. His crinkly face squished against his pillow, and then he closed his eyes and fell asleep.

FOURTEEN

—

Mrs. Gorham dreamed. She sprinted inland faster
than her old bones would allow. Sand churned beneath
her feet, along with the tiny feet of mice, the hooves
of deer, the paws of a wolf, the steady-beating wings
of ravens and seagulls and chickadees. She ran, her
own feet turning to those of the deer and her arms
becoming that of the raven. A storm would land soon,
and she refused to be caught out when it arrived.

The ocean regularly remade the outline of the Cape,
pushing and pulling at the sand and rocks of the

coastline, changing the contours of its bent-arm shape. Eliza felt as if her life were the Cape and Dire's bargains were the ocean, tugging and tugging until Eliza would give way and alter form.

She spent the night staring at a crack that ran from the light fixture outward, branching at a point to form a Y. She followed the path of the break and her thoughts spun into a tight whirlwind. She couldn't sleep, and she couldn't draw in a full breath, and she couldn't force the sense off her chest that everything she thought she'd known was a lie.

One, two, three. She looked over at Winnie.

One hundred and twenty-three, one hundred and twenty-four, one hundred and twenty-five. She reminded herself that her sister was still here, still safe.

One hundred and seventy-nine, one hundred and eighty, one hundred and eighty-one. Her heartbeat didn't slow; the feeling didn't pass.

Sunday arrived with a sleepless headache knotting in Eliza's skull. Her throat stayed half-closed, an impossible tube to breathe through. Her insides didn't seem to match her outsides, and she wasn't sure how to refit the pieces so they locked tight. The phone rang just as she climbed from bed. It was Mrs. Gorham on the party line, passing along the news that school was closed until further notice. This time, it wasn't because someone died, but rather because a rotted tree fell during the night and collapsed the schoolhouse's roof.

"How's Miss Alayna?" Pa said, holding the phone at an angle so the entire Serling family could hear.

"Upset," said Basil Hardwick. "I've convinced her to stay at our place, in Bri's old room, until we fix up the schoolhouse. It'll be a busy few days with clearing the tree and repairing the roof."

Pa sighed and tapped his forehead with the phone receiver. "I'll get my things," and said, and then hung up. A muscle ticked in his jaw.

Eliza couldn't look him in the face.

"You two can help," Pa said. "You'll clear branches and—"

The phone rang again, shrill and angry so close to their heads.

"What is it?" Pa said into the line after wrenching the receiver free.

"Hello?" said the Gorhams.

"Hello?" said Mr. Hardwick.

"Hello," said the Nye brother who lived up Old Queen Mae.

"It's me," said Zilpha.

At her aunt's voice, Eliza stood on her tip toes and shouted, "Hi! Hi, Zilpha. Haven't seen you in ages."

Pa looked at her sideways, but she ignored this. Zilpha and she had talked only a little on the drive home from the library, with Zilpha asking very few questions. No questions, really.

"I can hear you, Eliza. Stop shouting," Zilpha said. "You're to help me clean today."

Click, click, went the phone line as the Gorhams, Hardwicks, and Nyes hung up.

"Dire phoned this morning. He's calling in the cleaning job I promised," Zilpha said.

Pa frowned hard at the phone.

"Let me go," Eliza whispered. If she saw Dire, maybe she could force information from him regarding Ma's bargain. "Let me go! You'll have enough other people helping with the schoolhouse. You don't need me."

Pa's gaze shifted to her.

"I'll be safe. I promise I will be. Nothing like what happened at the ocean. Besides, Zilpha will watch over me. You know Dire won't dare try anything tricky with her around."

Zilpha coughed, though it sounded an awful lot like a laugh. "I promise, Waylon. I won't let Dire try anything tricky. Besides, he might not even be around. He likes taking long walks on the beach after it storms out."

Pa grimaced. "I didn't need to know that. Fine. Fine, Eliza can go, but you keep her away from him."

"Good, and Winnie can stay with you," Zilpha said. "She can help with town cleanup."

"Winnie should come with us." Eliza grasped Winnie's hand. "I can watch her *and* clean."

"Winnie can stay on her own just fine," Winnie said, going cross-eyed as her gaze swung between Eliza and Pa.

"Filemon can watch Winnie," said another voice on the line, and it took Eliza a moment to understand that Mr. Hardwick hadn't hung up his phone like she'd assumed.

Pa nodded, then: "Right. That'll do. I'll bring Winnie to stay with Filemon for the day. Eliza will wait for Zilpha to pick her up at the Jester." He hung up and disappeared to gather the tools needed to help clear the tree and start repairing the schoolhouse.

Eliza couldn't unfasten her hand from Winnie's. Why would Zilpha take Winnie from her after what happened the other night? She couldn't rid herself of the image of Winnie holding both hands out to the Wolf in the library, as if offering herself up.

At least Filemon would be there to watch her.

Winnie pulled away from Eliza and slid down the wall beside the phone and slumped until she sat on her haunches, feet scooted close to her bottom. "I'm always left out."

"You're never left out. You always go everywhere with everyone," Eliza said. "Come on, finish your oatmeal so you're ready to leave with Pa."

"I'm tired of oats," she muttered.

"Unless you want to eat leftover cod, you need to eat the oats." Eliza crossed around the bar and went to the mattress Mr. Chess had slept on. Before leaving in the middle of the night, he'd folded his quilt into a crisp square. She propped the mattress against the wall leading to the stairs, knowing Pa could haul it up there easier than she, and crossed back to pick up Winnie's strewn sheets. Two white-and-gray-splotched feathers tumbled off her pillow to decorate the floor. She picked them up and held both to the window, letting light shine through them, but then in a rush, she tossed both into the fire where they quickly burned. Wiping her hands on her dress, she told herself to check the attic for an owl nest later, in case that's where Winnie kept picking them up.

Pa and Winnie headed into the day. Sunlight poured out of the spotless, blue sky, and Eliza squinted at it, angry at the way the warmth made her head ache in the space behind her eyes. Sweat slid down her sides, and she peeled off her light coat, hanging it over the Jester's door handle. She'd be like Zilpha today with her sleeves rolled up, impervious to the chill winter air.

When Zilpha arrived, she leaned out the motorcar window and eyed Eliza. "It's happening, isn't it?"

"What's happening?"

"Where's your coat?"

"I got hot with the sun out."

"It's still cold out, Eliza."

"It doesn't feel like it." She'd been hot since…well, for days now. Had it been since falling into the ocean? Likely something to do with the cold water messing with her nerves.

"Go get it. You might want it later."

Eliza folded her hands in front of her belly, pressing her fingers down hard. "We're going to be working all day. I don't want to sweat inside it and then freeze if a wind comes up."

"Still. I don't like it. Get your coat and throw it in the back. No—no arguing. I'm still your elder."

Eliza did as she was told, feeling small and insignificant and incapable of making decisions for herself. Worry lines stretched tight over Zilpha's face, reaching into her hairline, blending into the few silvered strands that threaded through her black hair, and making Eliza believe that she was more upset over last night's events than she'd let on. She couldn't possibly be this troubled by Eliza not wanting to wear a coat. Eliza tossed her jacket into the motorcar and climbed into the passenger seat. There, she tucked her hands beneath her legs, and Zilpha took off, pushing the motorcar as fast as it could go without skidding against wet rain puddles in the road.

Eliza stuck her head out of the car, letting wind suck at her hair and whip it around. She closed her eyes. Leaned her cheek against the back of one hand. Listened to the gallop of wind. Allowed it to twist into the spill of waves at the ocean's surface. An echoing ache started in the hollow space of her lungs.

Thirty-one, thirty-two, thirty-three. The ache didn't melt away as it should.

Two hundred and one, two hundred and two, two hundred and three. Instead, it multiplied, filling up the cavern inside her rib cage.

Three hundred and twelve, three hundred and thirteen, three hundred and fourteen. Knuckles pressed to sternum, she pushed hard, trying to shove back the feeling that she was dying.

"You all right?" Zilpha asked. "You're looking peaky."

Eliza took a breath and then four more, refilling her body with oxygen and steeling herself before looking at Zilpha. Her aunt watched her more than the road. "I'm tired is all. I didn't sleep after we got home."

"Bad dreams?"

"I never dream."

Zilpha snorted. The motorcar turned down road after road, taking them the back way, pulling them east across Cape Fen and into Rio, and then onto the tip of the Cape where water expanded on three sides around them—Fen Bay to their west and the ocean to the north and east. Eliza sat forward in the seat with her palms pushed against the dash. *Oh!* She felt pulled forward, as if the motorcar wasn't blocking her, she would tip over into the water and become part of it.

She turned her thoughts to last night, to Sheriff Olavi's appearance and the Wolf and to Zilpha finding them. "How did you know where we were last night?"

Zilpha talked over the wind. "You have to understand. My sister made me promise to watch over you before she left. I wasn't happy about it at the time, because I didn't want her to go, but I agreed. I loved her. I would've agreed to anything to make her happy."

Eliza stared at ocean, refusing to blink, as this new information rooted inside her. Zilpha had known Eliza's mother was going to leave? Had she known about the bargain Ma made?

"I'm always listening for you, Eliza. Always." Zilpha gripped the steering wheel tight. "Truthfully, Dire didn't call in the cleaning job this morning, but after last night, I had a feeling you'd need to see him, though I was honest when I told your pa that I don't know if Dire'll be home or not. He really does like to walk the beach after it storms."

Zilpha took a right at the fork, branching away from Dire's lighthouse and toward his manor. A wooden fence trailed alongside the drive, leading up and over the gently swelling landscape of hills and tall, winter-dead grass. The two-story hall loomed up, not nearly as large as Eliza would have thought it to be, but still big enough that five families the size of the Serlings could live in it comfortably.

They parked the motorcar, took out their cleaning gear, and headed to the front. Zilpha knocked and called for Dire, but no footsteps echoed from inside. She tried the knob, and the door swung open.

"Hello? Dire?" she called, but the man didn't appear.

Tension wound tight in Eliza. If Dire was here, she could confront him sooner rather than later, but if he wasn't here, she could comb his house for clues. Maybe Dire kept records of his bargains the way Pa kept records of the ingredients that went into his sleeping draught.

She followed after Zilpha, stepping over the threshold and into a cavernous chamber. The sharp lines of the wall led up and up and up, finally meeting black ceiling tiles that swirled in a dizzying pattern. To their right was a stairwell that rose to the second floor, where a balcony hovered, likely connecting sleeping rooms from one side of the house to the rooms on the other. Directly to their right on the other side of the stairwell was a room with a grand piano pressed against the wall and sitting chairs surrounding it, as if Dire was prepared to hold a concert. Ma had made Eliza take lessons years before from Mrs. Gorham, but she'd played on an upright piano. She'd never seen such a large piano, its lid raised to show the strings beneath. In front of them was a room filled with a flower-patterned couch, lush chairs on either end, and a record player in one corner. Bookcases and black-and-white photographs lined the walls. In one, Dire stood behind two women, his hands placed on both their shoulders. Severe expressions crossed their faces, and as Eliza inched forward, she noticed that all three had one black eye and one clouded white.

"Dire's mother and grandmother," Zilpha said from behind her.

"Did you know them?" Eliza asked.

"I did. They were interesting women." Zilpha turned her back to the photograph and eyed the room. "I used to spend nearly the whole of my winters here. Dire's mother always welcomed me in her home… He's changed the furniture around."

Eliza didn't know what to do with the thought that her aunt had once spent so much time in the three witches' company as to have memorized the layout of the furniture. "Mr. Chess said that Dire's bad at magic and that it doesn't ever go the way people think it'll go."

Zilpha huffed out a breath. "It's less that Dire's bad at magic, and more that he never practiced. He didn't ask to learn from his grandmother when she was alive, because he foolishly assumed his mother would be around to teach him. When his mother passed away suddenly, it became apparent he would have to learn magic on his own. It was difficult for him."

"How do you know all this?"

A small smile played at the corners of Zilpha's mouth. "I knew Dire very well during that time. Once, I thought I might marry him."

Eliza turned away from Zilpha's smile. She didn't know what to do with the knowledge that had things been different, Zilpha might have married Dire, and Eliza might have witch cousins. Instead of saying this, she said, "His house is cozier than I would've thought."

"He's always liked comfort."

"He could host parties here." Eliza thought of her own family who *lived* in the kitchen for half the year, and indeed, when she took a hall that branched to the left, she found an expansive room containing a long, oak table at which she counted twenty chairs padded with velvety white fabric.

She took another turn and discovered the kitchen, complete with a beautifully wrought stove, but Zilpha stopped her before she could enter and wander more. They made a plan: Eliza would clean the upstairs of the manor with Zilpha taking the bottom. Eliza left the kitchen, backtracked through the hall, and went upstairs. Turning right, she opened the first of two closed-off rooms. The door swung open, and she waved her hands into the darkness of the room beyond. *Just a room; it's just a room*, she repeated in her head as she maneuvered into the cold darkness with hands and arms spread wide. The knuckles on her right hand smacked into a wall. She winced and stuck them in her mouth to calm the unexpected pain, then used the wall to find the windows. When she tugged back the heavy blinds that hung over the glass, her breath dropped out of her.

The ocean spread before her. She didn't have to look down to know the manor butted up against the edge of a cliff. If she would swing open the window and step out, she would sail off into the air to fall to the water below. She turned her head to press her ear against the glass, and—*there*—she closed her eyes and listened. *Whoosh, crash, floosh.* Ocean waves smashed against the rocks below.

She pressed her forehead and palms against the window, the world about her turning into a haze. Steam spiraled from her mouth, fogging the glass and slicking into her face. The distant boom of tireless waves meeting rock washed into her ears and swept into her bones. The yearning at her core deepened. Time slipped by.

The two pieces of her drifted apart. One was Eliza, with fingers clenched tight, grappling with the version of her that used to exist when Ma was around. That part of her dove beneath water to touch the ocean floor, fell into awe at the might of the waves, and felt safe within the ocean's waters. She'd tried so hard to get rid of that part of her, and now, she struggled to stuff herself whole, and to stitch back together the seams she'd sewn over the past four years.

A sound cracked behind her; Zilpha shook out blinds somewhere on the first floor. Heart thumping wildly, Eliza wrenched the curtains back in place and flung the room into black. She gulped in air and wiped sweaty palms against her shirt.

I am one person. I am Eliza, she said, and tore herself away, leaving behind a piece of her in the condensation on the glass. She felt her way toward the door, searching again for the light switch. The bulb in the ceiling turned on with a soft *whump* and a yellowing glow illuminated the space, far safer than the bright sunlight outside.

Knowing that busy hands made for a calm mind, she swept the room, wiped down the baseboards, aired out the armoire, shook out the sheets on the soft bed surrounded by dark-stained wood, dusted the nightside tables, and organized the books stacked on top of the dresser. When she reached the window, she squeezed her eyes shut and wiped away the smudges left by her nose and fingerprints without looking.

She cleaned the second room much the same way, and then headed across the balcony, keeping her sight line trained on the tread of her feet. There were two doors on this side of the house as well. The first handle she tried was locked. Was this Dire's private room? She wiggled the handle, then leaned down to peer at the lock. Could she pick it? She'd never picked a lock before, but that wouldn't stop her from trying. She imagined if Dire had secrets hidden in his home, they lived behind this door. She scrounged through her cleaning tools, but only found cloths and bottles of cleaning sprays, nothing that resembled a key or piece of metal with which to force open a lock. Frustrated, she rattled the handle and pressed her shoulder against the door to see how much it might give. But this was no flimsy, hollowed out piece of wood. This was a slab of heavy cedar that didn't give way beneath Eliza's weight.

She took a step back and raised one leg; she would smash the lock with her foot and risk both Dire and Zilpha's fury if it meant saving Winnie. She reared back, knee lifting to her chest—

A click sounded.

She froze.

The door handle turned, and the door swung back to reveal Dire, standing with one hand in a pocket and the other on the door knob. Long hair, the same shade of white as Winnie's, stayed tucked behind his ears. Up close, she could see that yes, one eye was black, and the other was clouded white. Just like the family portrait downstairs.

"Hello." He put both hands in his trouser pockets, standing loose and easy, as if he were nothing but curious about her presence in his home. "I was beginning to think you wouldn't come."

"We've been here for hours," Eliza said, settling the folds of her dress over her ankles, as if she'd never thought to kick down his door.

"I hadn't heard. I've been working."

Working on magic? Eliza wanted to ask.

Dire grinned. "Nothing with magic. I've been writing letters. Sheriff Olavi hasn't let up with her investigation, even though Kendare died of drowning."

"Drowning in air," Eliza said, repeating what Mrs. Chess had told her, even though she didn't know what it meant.

"It really is too bad, isn't it?" Dire patted his pocket. "Hopefully the letters will clear up any confusion over my part in things, but I'll have to send them to Olavi later. For now, you have questions for me."

Eliza fisted her hands to stop from covering her ears with her palms—she felt as if he could hear her thoughts.

Dire cocked his head to the side. "You look different than when I last saw you."

"I saw you only a day ago."

"Still, something's changed."

Eliza's skin tingled. The mismatched parts of her grated against one another. "Nothing's changed about me."

"If you say so." He fiddled with the clasps on the cuffs of his jacket, a crease forming high on his forehead. "While you're here, would you like to play a game?"

"I don't play games."

"That's as silly as saying you don't dream."

"I don't dream, either."

"Everyone dreams."

"Not me."

"You lie, though. Liars are always good at dreaming."

"I'm *not* lying."

"Not even now?"

Eliza's gaze snapped up and met Dire's clouded eye. It reminded her of a winter storm. She got the feeling that even now as they spoke, he was playing a game, and she didn't like it. She didn't know the rules of whatever game it was he played.

"How about this," Dire said. "We'll play a card game, and if you win, I'll give you a truthful answer to any question you'd like."

"I don't trust you enough that you'll tell the truth," Eliza said.

"I will if you win."

"What happens if I lose?"

Dire shrugged. "No consequences."

She didn't believe him, but she *did* believe she should take the chance. "I'll play a game, but this isn't a bargain. I'm not letting you trap me in something."

"I never trap anyone in anything." He led her from the balcony, down the stairs, and back to the kitchen. They walked past an island covered in a shiny, white rock. A small bowl rested in the middle, and in the center of it were pressed flowers: delicate purple lilacs the size of her thumb. She tore her gaze from the flowers and noticed a cast-iron pot with a towel thrown over it. When she breathed in, the kitchen smelled of fresh bread and warmth. She passed by cabinets and cookery and cutlery, a fancy gas-powered stove and range, and an electric refrigerator she had only ever heard rumors of but had never seen. She clenched her fingers to stop herself from tugging it open and seeing how cold its insides were. They stopped beside a heavy wooden table that butted against full-length windows on the far side of the room. She forced herself not to look down to the ocean and sat with her back to the view. *No,* she said to it, even when it set invisible fishing hooks into the back of her spine and tried to reel her in. *No.*

"Kings and Queens?" Eliza asked, in an attempt to distract herself. Dire laid out cards. The strategy game was a pastime everyone on Cape Fen played during winter when storms and snow kept them bundled inside.

"I've always liked the game, though I rarely have anyone to play with," Dire said. It seemed as if something shifted beneath his skin. He was the night sky midwinter when northern lights danced across the darkness. She tried to avoid it, but she glanced again into his clouded eye, and an echo of sorrow reached her.

She remembered something Miss Alayna had said in

school: *The light from stars is millions of years old, reaching us eons after they've burned out.*

It was as if Eliza were seeing Dire from very far away.

He turned to his cards, hiding away his clouded gaze, and Eliza found it much easier to hate him when she couldn't imagine sadness in his face. She took her pile of cards and held them fanned near her chest. She shuffled them, arranging each to allow for easy access later and was happy to see a Queen of Spades already resting in her grip. She'd been gifted a good hand.

"I want to know why Ma set a bargain on Winnie," she said.

Dire's brows rose.

"I'm preparing you for when I win." There was no choice but for her to win. "I want to know what the bargain was and how to stop it. Your Wolf can't have my sister."

"I'm not sure I understand."

"Your Wolf tried to eat Winnie! And if your Wolf tried to eat her, it means someone—probably Ma—struck a bargain with her as the cost."

Dire's chin tucked down, and he laughed, laughed hard enough that his hair fell from behind his ears to cover his face. "Oh dear." He wiped his cheeks where tears leaked from his eyes. "Oh *dear*. How right and how wrong you are. I will have to have a word with my Wolf when I see it next."

Rage spiraled through Eliza at his laughter. None of this was funny.

Dire drew from the pile on his right and shuffled it into his cards. He set one elbow on the table and rested chin in hand, a happy smile on his face and touching his eyes. His smile widened when he noticed Eliza's scrutiny. "This is nice."

"It's *not*," she managed to say.

His smile dropped away. A smidgen of regret sounded in Eliza. She stomped it down and instead focused on *Winnie* and on the bargains Dire wielded. That he held such power made her furious, and this fury made words loose and sharp in her mouth: "Tell me about Winnie."

Dire flattened his cards on the table. "This is all anyone ever wants from me. Bargains and answers to questions I have no right or ability to tell."

"You're the bargainer. You can do whatever you like."

"How I wish that were so." Dire tapped the back of his cards, then picked them up and fanned them out with his long fingers. "I cannot tell you anything specific about the bargain, but perhaps I can tell you the when. You and your sister's birthdays are one week apart, correct? That means yours will be in a few days. *That* is your when."

"My birthday?"

"You'll be twelve, and Winnie will be eight and one week

old…or not, if the bargain comes to pass. That's your when, Eliza Serling."

"Why does my birthday matter?"

"That is an excellent question. Is that the question you would like answered, if you win?"

"No!"

"Not that you've won." Dire leaned back.

Eliza looked down. Four queens were set before Dire, but—

"You cheated!" She pulled the Queen of Spades from the cards in her hand and shoved it at him.

"I never set any rules," Dire said.

"Decks of cards aren't supposed to have two Queens of Spades. They only have one."

Dire picked up the card Eliza held out. He ran his fingers over it and when he flipped it toward her, she saw it was only a *king*. A King of Spades. It didn't make sense.

Dire said, "That was a very pleasant game. Come by to play again sometime."

She gripped the edge of the counter, knuckles bleaching white and red. "I won't ever! You—" A hand grasped the side of her neck, cutting off her words. Eliza jerked back, startled to see her aunt behind her.

"We'll take our leave now," Zilpha said.

"No. He cheated!" Eliza shouted.

"Thank you, Dire."

"But, Zilpha!"

"Eliza, get your things. Winnie and your father will expect us home soon." Zilpha pulled on the back of Eliza's shirt, hauling her off the stool and toward the doorway.

Eliza tossed the rest of her cards on the floor and rushed out of the kitchen, storming harder than the skies had the night before. She headed upstairs to the balcony where she'd left her bucket of cleaning supplies. There she paused at the top of the landing because—as she well knew—sound traveled. *Voices* traveled. Low, harsh arguments spiraled through space to fill the cavern that was Dire's welcoming living room.

"You know I can't do that," Dire said. "She's not yours to bargain away."

Zilpha's response came sharp and angry, "I'm not bargaining her *away*, I'm bargaining *for* her. For her life."

"That will cost you more. It always does."

"*She's turning into an animal!*"

"Eliza's birthday is only a few days away. She might make it."

"You know she won't, you devil." Zilpha's footsteps clattered from the kitchen, and Eliza hurried back to the first floor.

"Please come back to visit!" Dire shouted from the kitchen. "My door is always open."

Zilpha hissed a retort. She snatched up Eliza's hand, dragged her from the house, and slammed the front door behind them. They climbed into Zilpha's motorcar. Zilpha cranked the engine, her motions sharp and angry as it sputtered to life. As soon as it started, she peeled down the drive, leaving Dire far behind.

"It was Winnie you were talking about, wasn't it? It's not possible. It's *not!*"

Zilpha swung the motorcar around at the fork in the road and slammed her bare foot into the gas. "Your birthday's Wednesday." Her shoulders tensed. "Hold out for a few more days, Eliza. Try for me, will you?"

Eliza fisted her hands in her skirts, twining the fabric tight around her fingers and shoving away any concern she might feel for herself. She wouldn't allow herself to be in danger. She had her sister to protect. "What about Winnie?"

Zilpha gripped the steering wheel.

"What about Winnie!"

"*I don't know!*"

Eliza bit her tongue, and Zilpha drove on.

FIFTEEN

Mr. Hardwick dreamed. Trees bent over him, limbs
grasping at his clothes and shoving him into the depth
of the dark woods. Orcas swam through the air, passing
through branches, flying and playing and singing
with their family. He missed his family—his wife
who had died and his son who had left. He struggled
through the forest to reach Filemon, continuing
on, even when twigs left scratches on his skin.

When Zilpha dropped Eliza off at the Jester, it was to
discover Sheriff Olavi sitting at the counter across from
Pa, eating a bowl of lentil soup. The bun at the nape of her neck

frizzed, as if she'd spent the day hurrying and hadn't had the chance to tidy up her hair.

"Baron Dire wrote letters to you," Eliza blurted. Her insides burned, even though she hadn't worn the thin coat Zilpha had made her take.

Sheriff Olavi sat up, pulling back her shoulders that had been hunched over her dinner. "And how do you know that?"

"I cleaned his house with Zilpha."

"Why were you cleaning *Dire's* house?"

Eliza wasn't about to tell Sheriff Olavi that she'd wanted to interrogate Dire. Not that it'd worked. Feeling defensive, she said, "Barons need their houses cleaned too."

"As if he's a real baron," Sheriff Olavi said. "He's not anything related to nobility. His grandmother stole the title!"

"*Olavi*," Pa said, low.

Sheriff Olavi sucked in a breath. She nodded once, then scraped the last dregs of soup from her bowl with a piece of bread and said. "You'll do as I asked?"

"I'm not as influential as you seem to think I am," Pa said.

"All the same." Sheriff Olavi took up her hat from where it sat on the counter and set it on her head, nice and straight. She patted Eliza's shoulder as she walked past and headed down the street into the night.

Eliza shut the door behind her. The fever setting her skin

afire made her fingers damp with sweat, leaving behind a thumb print on the metal doorknob. She wiped her hands on her dress, praying Pa wouldn't notice. If he noticed, he'd ask what was wrong, and she'd have to admit she didn't know. She didn't feel as if she were getting sick, but still—

"Did cleaning Dire's house go well?" Pa asked.

Eliza looked at him, remembering him as he'd been before Ma left. He'd smiled a lot, and the restaurant hadn't closed in winter. Everyone in town would stop by during the week, passing on gossip and buying bottles of Ma's sleeping draught, especially if they'd bargained with Dire and had a difficult time sleeping dreamless on their own. Pa *had* been influential, but at some point, that had stopped being important to him.

"Eliza?"

Cleaning Dire's house had gone terribly. She said, "It went okay. How did fixing the schoolhouse go?"

"Well enough. It'll take more time to finish the roofing."

"Oh," Eliza said, feeling bad for Miss Alayna, and also feeling bad for Filemon and the niece or nephew he would have soon.

Pa nodded, looking as if he wanted to say more. Instead, he handed her dinner bowls to clean. Eliza headed into the kitchen and found Winnie standing on the countertop, one ear pressed to the wall.

"Sheriff's gone?" Winnie asked. "Pa said I had to stay back here while they talked about 'adult things', but he didn't tell me I couldn't listen."

Colby had been right; eavesdropping came natural to the Parletts. "Did you hear anything good?"

"'Adult things' meant stuff about the Wolf. Sheriff wants to make a hunting party to catch the Wolf and run Dire out of town. She wants him gone."

"If Dire leaves, we might all find a way to be free," Eliza said as she helped Winnie off the counter. If everyone would be free, it meant she and Winnie could find Ma on the continent, and it meant Pa would stop being so sad. The thought of it fluttered inside her lungs.

Winnie shrugged. "They didn't say anything about that."

Eliza's fingers snagged on the back of Winnie's head where the snarl had gotten worse. Strands of hair clung to her sweaty palms. A shudder went through her. She had to admit at last that it was no use trying to untangle it. She may not have answers to most of her questions, but she could fix this one small problem.

She asked, "Are you ready for a haircut?"

Winnie flopped her arms at her side. "I've been asking for one for six hundred years!"

"Four days!" Eliza laughed, tension releasing inside her at her sister's exaggeration. "You've only had the knot for four days."

She shook off any last nerves or thoughts that she'd failed Winnie somehow by not having taken care of her better, found Pa's silver scissors, and set Winnie before the fire where she could feed locks of hair to the flame. Wiping her hands on the bottom of her skirts, she smoothed them over Winnie's head. Her sister smelled of the night sky. Of stars and the moon and the sort of darkness that birthed dreams. It was fresh and sweet, almost like the birthday butter cookies Winnie loved so much.

"Maybe Pa would let us climb onto the roof and watch the stars tonight," Eliza said. "You'd like that."

"Could we bring a snack?" Winnie asked.

"Didn't you just eat dinner?"

"Yes, but I'd like a snack too." She looked back at Eliza, her eyes the same shade of black as the silent witching hour her mother used to speak of: *It's the most wondrous time of the night, when the best dreams are brewed. Careful of it, Eliza.*

Eliza shoved away thoughts of Ma and made Winnie turn her head. *Snip, snip.* Fine white hair dusted Winnie's shoulders and fell to the floor. Eliza cut in a straight line at the base of her skull, shearing off six inches of hair. The knot had grown to the size of a golf ball, and it resisted the scissors, almost as if Eliza were trying to cut through tree bark or a skein of yarn or a damp fishing net.

Eliza called, "Pa, we need to sharpen your scissor—"

The lump severed in half. A chunk of hair dropped into Eliza's lap. What hair remained at Winnie's neck unspooled, and from between the strands, a white and gray feather emerged.

One. Eliza stopped breathing.

Two. She pulled the feather, tugging when it didn't come loose.

Three. She wrenched hard, yanking it free and causing Winnie to cry out and clap a hand to her scalp. Winnie spun on her knees, facing Eliza with fury tightening her brow.

Four. She set the feather on the floor, not tossing it to the fire as she had all the others.

Five. She cradled Winnie's face between her clammy hands.

"I keep finding them everywhere I go," Winnie whispered.

Eliza breathed. *In, out, in, out.* But her racing heart refused to slow.

"Hoot, hoot."

Fear trembled out of Eliza's mouth along with her words, "It came out of you…out of your head. How long has that been happening?"

"Six hundred years." A too-wide, panicked grin stretched across Winnie's mouth.

"Four days? *Four days* feathers have been falling out of your head and you didn't tell me?"

"I didn't know they were coming out of my head. I've just

been finding them. They were on my pillow and on the floor and outside and everywhere." Winnie pulled away from Eliza's grip. She scrubbed her fingers through her hair, tugging at the chin-length locks. Scrubbing and tugging and scrubbing and tugging until another feather tumbled to the floor.

Desperately, Eliza scratched at the roots of Winnie's hair, finding little downy feathers hidden along her scalp. The fluff of it smoothed against Eliza's skin, fuzzy and newborn-owlet soft.

"What's happening?" Winnie said, hiccupping as tears pooled in her eyes and streamed down her cheeks.

She's turning into an animal! Zilpha had shouted at Dire.

"You're okay. It's okay," Eliza said, lying to make Winnie feel better, even though everything had gone horribly wrong. She forced herself to stop touching Winnie's hair and pressed her cheek to her sister's. "*It's okay.* I promise I'll figure this out. I'll fix everything."

"It hurts," Winnie whimpered. She grabbed up the fallen feathers on the floor and scrunched them in her fists. "It feels like I'm tearing in half. I'm two. It feels like I'm *two*."

Eliza pulled back, her aching hands frozen in midair.

"There are two of me!"

The two parts of Eliza that had pushed farther apart at Dire's house chafed against one another. They pressed against her skin, warming her insides. She spread her fingers wide, feeling an invisible tug between each finger, a web of skin she couldn't see. "*Winnie*. There are two of me too."

Winnie sucked in her lips. Her tears stopped flowing, though one trembled on the edge of her nose. Eliza dabbed it away. It felt as if she'd sunk into a shadow with her sister, as if together, they'd stepped onto the dark side of the moon. Up there, spinning outside the earth, Eliza saw not two sisters, but four. Two Elizas and two Winnies. And from off the back of Winnie's head, feathers scattered.

"What's happening?" Winnie asked.

I don't know, Eliza thought to say, though she dared not admit it aloud.

Eliza's insides heated, scalding her until she sweated beneath her thin clothes. All the scents around the Jester intensified: the Wolf who had walked circles around their home, Pa's sleeping draught, the soup Pa had made, small mice that had made a home in their attic, and Winnie—pine trees and ocean fog and columns of warm air meant to lift birds into the sky.

"I brought the sharpening stone for the scissors," Pa said from the doorway. "Eliza? *Winnie?*"

Eliza spun, doing her best to hide Winnie and the feathers behind her, but one glance at Pa's face and she knew it was too late.

Pa stood at the door, gripping the frame with one hand and holding the whetstone with the other. Red rimmed his eyes. "What's happening?"

Eliza's fists shook at her sides, as all of her confusion burst free. "Ma made a bargain. Dire told me so. He said it ends on my birthday. *You* said not to worry! You said Winnie should be safe. Well, she's *not* safe. She has feathers coming out of her head. That's the opposite of safe!"

Pa squeezed his eyes shut, wrinkles puckering across the weathered skin of his face.

"What bargain was it?" Eliza forced out. "What bargain did Ma make? Why does Winnie have feathers in her hair? Why did Ma bargain Winnie away and not *me*?"

Here was the awful truth of it—why would Ma have let Winnie be hurt? Of all of them, Winnie was the most precious.

Winnie tugged at the back of Eliza's dress. "It shouldn't be you either, Liza."

Eliza couldn't look at her, not because of the strange feathers lining her scalp, but because of the first time the Wolf had attacked. Eliza had tried to sacrifice herself then, and Winnie had stared at her with a cross, *how dare you* expression. Eliza couldn't stand it if that's how Win looked at her now too.

Pa deflated in the center. His chest turned bowl-shaped and shoulders drooped and head fell forward, and really—this was not her pa. "I told you Winnie wasn't the cost of anyone's bargain. That's not possible. No one can bargain anyone else away. But you can bargain *for* someone, placing the cost on yourself."

"Mrs. Chess said that, but I don't understand."

"It's what Mr. Chess was telling us—he bargained *for* his wife, placing the cost of the new bargain on himself." Pa met her gaze, and Eliza found herself caught there—snagged in the same sorrow she'd seen reflected in Dire's eyes earlier that night. "The only bargain I know your mother made happened a long time ago, Eliza. Before you were born."

"But then why did she leave on my birthday? Did she bargain again?" *Two bargains?* Her ma had made two bargains?

"No." Winnie spoke from behind her. "Momma didn't leave."

Eliza steeled herself. The pain of the story wrapped tight inside her. She tested the truth of it, letting it burn her as it always did when she remembered. "Ma rowed into the ocean, Win. She rowed away on my birthday and left us."

"She did not! She disappeared."

"She took a rowboat into the bay, and she didn't come back. She *left*."

"*No!*" Winnie stomped both her feet. Her chest rose and fell rapidly and her cheeks burned red.

Eliza reached for her, but she darted away. This wasn't a conversation they'd ever had as a family. They hid their secrets; they didn't share things like the Hardwicks. Eliza closed her open hand and let it rest at her side, remembering Filemon's easy friendship and the truth that existed between him and his Pa, even when it caused them pain. Even if it hurt, Eliza wanted that same understanding. She wouldn't lie anymore. Not to Winnie. Not to Pa.

"I don't know what's happening," she said. "I don't know why you're growing feathers or what the bargains were or how to stop them, but I do remember Ma rowing across the ocean. I know she's on the continent somewhere."

"You know she's gone," Winnie said. "You remember all that, but I remember Ma rowing into the bay to catch fish. I remember sitting on the beach while she fished and you swam. After dinner and presents and cookies, she cleaned up, then went out into the street and disappeared. I saw it through the window. I remember."

Eliza's truth and Winnie's truth were not the same. They both held different pieces to the same puzzle. She said, "I'd gotten sick. I ate too many cookies." Her knees gave out. She thumped into a chair. She remembered eating butter cookies until her stomach expanded, nearly pushing the food back up her throat. She'd fallen asleep early and in the morning, Ma had been gone. Everything had blended together until it'd become a confused mess.

"She *poofed*," Winnie said. "She was there, then not."

Eliza's breath grew short. She didn't know where to put the sudden hope that lit inside her. If Ma poof-disappeared, then her bargain couldn't have been like Bri Hardwick's. Bri had swapped places with Miss Alayna and their baby, and he'd walked straight over the bridge to the continent. He certainly hadn't poof-disappeared.

"What do you remember, Pa? Please," Eliza said.

Pa ran his hands over his cheeks, then said, "It was all for you. Your mother said she bargained for you. That's all I know, I'm sorry."

PART III

—

IN WHICH THERE
IS A BARGAIN

SIXTEEN

—

Baron Dire dreamed. He tipped his face toward the
haunting moon. She'd pricked silver hooks into the
sky and towed them into her favorite hour when
the sun was fully on the opposite side of the world.
Wind hissed against dead leaves hanging from
sleeping trees. Ocean waves crashed against the
cliffs on the far side of the home his grandmother
once stole from a baron. Night scraped against Cape
Fen. And all of it shaped a dream in Dire's ear.

I n the end, Pa said nothing more about Ma's bargain or why
Winnie had feathers hidden among her hair. Either he

couldn't tell more of what he knew, or he wouldn't. The frustration of this gnawed at Eliza. There wasn't much she could do about it though, at least not now when bedtime called and when a funeral would take place in the morning.

On Monday, in honor of Kendare's life, Fenians dressed in shades of gray that matched the gloom of the wintry sky and gathered on the beach of Fen Bay, exactly where Kendare's body had been discovered. A sun burned at Eliza's core, and so she wore only a thin cloak over her gray dress. Her body felt thick and sensitive, as if the night had lined the inside of her skin with heated water. Even her toes ached. Her feet wouldn't quite lace into her boots, and so she'd left them loose and floppy. It was like her body knew there were two versions of her trying to fit inside one frame.

One, two, three. Eliza held herself together with teeth clenched and arms held away from her sides.

Twenty-two, twenty-three, twenty-four. She refused to fall apart now.

Fifty-one, fifty-two, fifty-three. Not with Winnie waking from sleep surrounded by molted feathers.

"She looks mad," Winnie said.

Eliza breathed and peeled her gaze from the ocean that she'd watched while her thoughts had drifted.

Winnie pointed at Loretta Parlett, their aunt and Kendare's wife. She wore a high-necked dress of gray flannel trimmed in storm-gray lace. Thick leather gloves covered her fisted hands, and wrinkles pleated the skin beside her lips. Her nose flared.

"She's definitely angry," Winnie said.

Loretta shook out her dress and tucked her chin against her collar, hiding from the sharp wind crossing the bay. Eliza had been to funerals before and had seen how anger could make a home at burial sites just as easily as sorrow. She noticed then that Sheriff Olavi stood behind Loretta. Red rimmed her eyes as well, though it was a slack-jawed red that reminded Eliza of Pa's face when insomnia made nights unbearable and days costly. Sheriff Olavi rubbed her face and turned to Lionel Parlett who stood at her elbow. He wore his hair in a crown of braids around his head, showing the way the brown strands were bleaching white at the roots. This was the strange thing about Lionel— come the change in season, his hair changed as well. In winter, it blended in with the white of snow, but in summer, it stayed a rich brown. Eliza didn't know if he dyed it, somehow, or if it had to do with Dire's magic.

Beside him, Colby folded her lace-covered arms over her chest. She glared at something in the distance. Eliza considered going to their cousin's side. She'd offered help before and might yet again, but with Lionel standing so close by, Eliza didn't dare.

She pulled Winnie against her side, ignoring the pang in her too-heated skin, and together they merged into the middle of the crowd. They found Filemon and the other kids from school, letting the adults around them block the wind.

Grease threaded the roots of Filemon's hair and shadows filled his cheeks, as if he hadn't slept or bathed since last they saw one another.

"You okay?" Eliza asked.

Filemon's brow furrowed. "Are you actually asking or are you just making conversation?"

"I'm asking."

He hesitated, then: "Bri called a bunch last night. Kept me up with the ringing. Dad was angry, especially after finding out I'd snuck into the library—"

"What—how?"

"I told. You know I can't lie to him. Besides, Grandma called saying the library had gotten messed up, probably with the Wolf running around and none of us remembering to lock the front door. Dad got the truth out of me pretty quick, after that."

"I'm sorry," Eliza said. "It's my fault. Things didn't turn out the way I expected."

Filemon's expression brightened. "They didn't turn out the way I expected either, but even though Dad was mad, I couldn't help but think it was the most exciting thing to have happened since Bri left."

"My sister almost getting eaten was exciting?"

"I didn't almost get eaten," Winnie muttered beside her. "I was fine."

Eliza started to say something more, but at that moment, Mr. Bodfish made his way through the crowd, stopping when he stood beside a rowboat half in, half out of the water.

Before them, the waves seemed to pause, as if drawing in a breath, and in that space, a baritone voice from somewhere behind them began to sing.

"*When night grows long, and to loneliness·I surrender, I look to thee, my softly growing dreams. Planted in a garden filled with splendor, unraveling my heart, my life, my being.*" All Fenians hushed, sinking into Mr. Chess's calming voice, listening as he reached the chorus. "*O rise my hope and take me to the sky. Help me to breathe. Help me to live. O rise my hope and take me to the sky. Carry me on to the grave.*"

No one had heard Mr. Chess sing since his disappearance. But now, he layered his voice in *Dreams to the Grave* as if wrapping the words in finery. As he sang, the crowd relaxed, and so did the angry lines of Loretta's face and the drooping shadows on Sheriff Olavi. Mr. Chess's voice wove through Eliza's mind and tugged loose strands of thought into a tapestry.

Pa had said Mr. Chess was trying to tell Eliza about bargains, that he'd bargained *for* Mrs. Chess. Because of it, he'd disappeared, and a year later he'd returned with no memory of where he'd been. Is this what had happened to Ma? Pa said she'd bargained *for* her daughters, and because of it, she'd disappeared. It had been more than a year though; it had been nearly *four* years, and she still hadn't returned. If she was going to come home, wouldn't she have done so by now?

Mr. Chess finished singing and Mr. Bodfish took his place, saying, "It is a tragedy when our beloved own leave us. It's with sadness and regret that we mourn the abrupt passing of Kendare Lovell. We're a family, on this Cape, and we'll bear this sorrow together, lifting up the Lovell family and assisting them as Kendare would have wanted. Loved by all, Kendare's loss will be felt across our lonely spit of land, particularly as winter has fully come upon us and as has been the case since Dire's grandmother first came to our Cape. We're all in this together. There's no other way to survive but to remember that we must support one another through the terrible trials life throws our way. So, we say goodbye to Kendare, for now. We wish him well on his journey in the afterlife."

Mr. Bodfish gestured to Loretta. She hoisted up the skirts of her mourning dress, revealing waders beneath, and slid into the choppy waves of the bay, followed closely by Mr. Bodfish and two other men. They splashed to the rowboat where Kendare's body lay and clambered over the edge. Mr. Bodfish took hold of the oars, digging one into the shallow waves to push off, and with a twist of his wrists and arms, began the trek out to sea.

They would cross the bay to arrive at Moorland Graveyard. Of course, they could take the road, but the bay's route was quicker, and it was tradition to allow the dead to pass over the waves one last time before being buried on the other side of the Cape.

A forlorn feeling steeled over Eliza. She stood on her tiptoes, trying to see between the bodies to watch the rowboat as it became a prick against the gray bay. She searched the waves for the boat, for the line over which Fenians couldn't cross. She searched for something she didn't quite have a name for. She took a step. Water sucked at her boots, swishing sand away beneath her feet.

"We don't have waders." Winnie twisted in her grip.

She took another step, her pulse stuttering loud in her ears and her feet heading toward the gray-black of the freezing ocean that would surely plummet the heat at her core.

"You get wet, you'll get hypothermia and die," Winnie said.

Eliza stepped into the depths of ice and the weight of waves and the caverns of land where fish and eels and sharks made their home, breathing water as she breathed air. *You can hold your breath, Eliza.*

"Stop, Liza!" Winnie plucked at Eliza's pinky finger, bending it back until a sharp pain radiated through her hand; Eliza released her hold on her sister, confused.

"I was—" Eliza rubbed the knuckle of her pinky. "I was just trying to see the boat."

Winnie folded her arms and squinted up. "Don't you be lying to me, Eliza Tynne Serling," she said.

"I'm not lying."

"Are too."

Eliza clamped her teeth shut, refusing to say *am not* back at Win. She looked back over the bay. Each of the ocean's feather-lipped waves caught behind her sternum. The water seemed to ask her something.

Yes, she wanted to say, though what the yes was in answer to, she didn't quite know.

Eliza took Winnie's hand and drew her after the crowd that swarmed toward town.

"We should stay away from the beach for a while," Winnie said, looking up at her and swinging her arms hard, as if she wanted to lift off the sand and fly.

Behind them, the water spoke to Eliza—it tasted of salt and fish and air, making hunger rumble in her belly. Longing pressed against the backs of her eyes.

"We should stay away," Winnie whispered. She'd stopped walking. Stopped swinging her arms. Stopped pretending flight.

"Right," Eliza said, eyeing Winnie's fluffy hair. "Yes."

To the invisible tethers that drew her toward the water, she said *no.*

No.

SEVENTEEN

—

Mr. Chess dreamed. He cupped one hand before his mouth and the other around his ear. He sang into the echo chamber made of his palms, the sweet melody chasing away his fear. His words tumbled free. "Don't let the devil inside you."

People spilled through the Fen Jester. The Serlings and Parletts might not get along, and her pa and Lionel might very well hate one another, but tradition meant the Jester always held after-funeral gatherings. Kendare's funeral was no different.

Eliza caught snippets of conversation as she walked through the Jester and filed it all away to sort through later.

"Does it matter what he bargained for? He's dead."

"It matters because we can learn from it. We can—"

"It *doesn't* matter."

"It does to me. I don't want to stumble into a bargain that ends up with me dead. So then, was his bargain about the ocean? About fish in the ocean? About the *tides* of the ocean?"

"Not even Kendare would be dumb enough to mess with the tides. He would need to have wished to become the moon to do that."

"Could make sense, seeing as how he's dead now. A big enough bargain might could kill a person."

Eliza wondered if perhaps Kendare had wished for control of the tides, if he sold his life to buy the workings of the moon. Or had Kendare done as her mother'd done and bargained *for* someone else and had given up his life to do so? She understood better now what a life was worth in one of Dire's bargains, and she believed the answer to be *not much*.

Eliza lifted a plate with cups of fizzy water and took them around the Fen Jester, careful not to drop it even though her hands ached. They were the same sort of sore as when she helped their neighbor churn milk into butter. Afterward, she'd stretch out her fingers and hear the joints snap with fatigue.

"I don't know about you," Mrs. Gorham said, "but I'm inclined to believe Kendare tried to be wily and slip out of his bargain altogether. Dire probably sent his Wolf to exact revenge."

"It's not right, speaking of the dead like this," said Mrs. Gorham's husband.

"He's the one who chose it. He's the one who made the bargain. He knew the consequences if he used his bargain in the wrong way. I've managed just fine—forty years of predicting weather, and Dire hasn't come for me once."

"Not everyone's as satisfied with the results of their bargain as you are. I'm tired of it all," Mr. Gorham said. "I'm tired of not knowing what will happen. To you. To our children. To our friends. I'm *tired*."

"We all are, dear, but there isn't much we can do about it." Mrs. Gorham leaned close to her husband, absentmindedly patting Eliza's head before pinching a glass off her tray.

Eliza ducked away, scowling.

"Kendare wished to be the moon—"

"Kendare wished for no winter—"

"Kendare wished to understand the ocean floor—"

"Kendare wished to catch fish in the deep bay waters—"

"Kendare wished to become a bargainer himself—"

But what little she could catch didn't include how bargains worked. All she heard were frustrations about the world, because clearly no one else understood either. The tray in her hand trembled as she clamped her fingers around the edge, too angry to think straight.

"None of them know what they're doing."

Eliza froze at the sound of Miss Alayna's voice.

"You realize that, don't you, Eliza? Everyone here assumes they know how bargains work because their family has lived here for a hundred years. No one is brave enough to admit they have no idea how Dire's magic works."

"I don't know how it works," Eliza said, not feeling brave at all for admitting it.

"You can admit to not knowing. You're a child. The truth gets more difficult to speak out loud the older you get." Miss Alayna sighed and leaned against her table, knocking over an empty glass and sending it rolling to the floor.

"I'll help," Eliza said, automatically picking it up so Miss Alayna didn't have to attempt it with her baby-filled belly getting in the way. "Ma always said being pregnant was a chore."

Miss Alayna snorted and looked at Eliza askance. "Your mother was never pregnant. I've heard the story enough times."

Eliza's mind blanked.

"I'm sorry." Miss Alayna grimaced. "I'm sorry. I shouldn't've said that. That was unfair of me."

"It's not true," Eliza said. "Why would you lie?"

"Eliza—"

"I'm not adopted. I'd know if I'd been adopted."

"I'm sorry, Eliza. You're right. It was a lie. I made it up," Miss Alayna said.

But that sounded like a lie too. A lie made up of lies, none of which Eliza could see through. She started to speak, but then her words dropped away as sound evaporated from the Jester. She turned in the direction Miss Alayna faced—in the direction everyone faced.

Baron Dire hovered in the doorway, framed by wintry light, tucking long strands of white hair behind his ears and roaming his one black eye and one clouded eye about the Jester.

"I heard there was a funeral," Dire said before shifting through the crowd and disappearing toward the counter.

The space behind Dire filled quickly, people moving in tight as if pulled by a vacuum, each craning their heads to peer over the crowd and mumble to their neighbors. Dire so rarely left his acreage on the point of the Cape.

"How dare he come here?" Sheriff Olavi stood behind Eliza, her face filling with furious, red blotches. "How *dare* he show up at a funeral he caused?"

"Kendare's the one who made the bargain, Olavi," Miss Alayna said.

"Dire didn't have to agree to it. He didn't have to set death on the table, now did he? He didn't have to send out his *Wolf*! He didn't have to *have* a wolf in the first place."

Eliza folded her arms and clenched her hands around her biceps to try to control the shudders that passed through her. She remembered Sheriff Olavi framed against the night, rifle pointed at the Wolf—almost at Winnie.

"You should ask him what Kendare bargained for," a Nye brother said.

"You think I haven't asked? Dire refuses to answer. He takes too much pleasure in his secrets," Sheriff Olavi said.

It hit Eliza then: *Dire was here.*

She turned away from Miss Alayna and Sheriff Olavi, her footsteps as dreamy as ocean foam. *Heel-toe, heel-toe, heel-toe,* she moved into the crowd, ducking below elbows and sneaking beside hips, careful not to bump or rattle anyone. She found Dire easily enough, right where the crowd was thickest. He was a magnet, or a rhubarb pie left on a counter to cool, or the sun—what had Miss Alayna said about the planets? He was gravity, tipping the world toward him, tumbling Fen into his rotation.

"*You cannot be here!*" A low, commanding voice stopped sound in the Jester for a second time. Pa's voice, his angry voice, his best-not-even-think-of-defying-me voice.

"But I *am* here," Dire said. "This is a funeral, and everyone on Cape Fen is invited. I am on Cape Fen, am I not?"

Eliza reached them. They stood behind the bar, one of Dire's hands holding the top of a bottle of sleeping draught and one of Pa's hands on the bottom, making it look as if they played tug-o-war with the tonic.

"There's no reason for you to be here." Fear showed in the whites of Pa's eyes.

"I've come to pay my respects."

"You've come to gloat!"

"Gloat? About what? One doesn't gloat at funerals."

"How should you know? You've never come to any!" Pa wrenched the bottle from Dire's grasp. His breath came out in angry exhalations. "Why now? Why bother coming here now?"

"You caused Kendare's death!" someone shouted from the crowd.

Dire recoiled, his eyelids closing against the accusation. "That wasn't my fault."

"If not yours, then whose?" Pa asked, harsh in tone and stance. "Get out. This is my restaurant. *Get out.*"

Dire glanced around the Jester, at the mass of people pressing together, glaring at him. He hesitated and crumpled in on himself. "Very well." He touched his brow and nodded at Pa before exiting the Jester in the exact same manner as he'd entered.

Eliza waited for Pa to become distracted and then bolted after Dire. Her nerves did a terrible sort of dance as she followed the stretch of his shadow across the frozen grass. He headed behind the Jester, though the only thing back there was Pa's shed. If Dire went in there, Pa was likely to murder him. Sure enough, he went inside. She followed, pulling open the door and eyes adjusting to the dimness inside. She located Dire's slender shape in the middle of the outbuilding. Something about the shadows reminded her of the Wolf standing beside Dire on the beach, and she found herself searching for it, even though she knew the Wolf couldn't come out during day.

"Hello." Dire reached out and brushed the top of a barrel. Black rings lined his fingers and made a quiet *clink* against the wood. "I had hoped your father would have extra bottles of his sleeping draught stored back here, but it seems he's hidden them away. I've begun to think I should try some. Rumors say it makes you sleep dreamless."

"I don't know why you need it."

"I don't ever truly sleep, Eliza. My nights cost me. All the dreams I ever hear are ones that belong to others, never myself."

Eliza didn't know if he was telling the truth or spinning a story, but either way, she knew Pa wouldn't like Dire stealing from him. "Pa will be mad if you take any."

"Yes, I realize that now." He sighed, a light and airy sound that reminded Eliza of a post-storm breeze. "It was nice having you stop by the other day." He reached behind another barrel, and when his hand reappeared, he held Winnie's wooden owl.

"Give that here!"

Dire offered the owl to her, and she snatched it away. The sore skin along her fingers throbbed when she clenched it in her hand and hid it in a pocket.

"I want to know about Ma," she said.

"Last time we met, you wanted to know about Winnie."

"I want to know about Ma *and* Winnie. Ma made a bargain, and I know Winnie's connected somehow."

"And you."

"Pa said that Ma bargained for both of us, but I don't believe it. There's no proof. I don't have feathers coming out of my head, and the Wolf's never wanted me." She clutched Winnie's owl, her fingers pressing hard against the wings.

"You're sure?"

"Yes! Tell me Ma's bargain!"

"I'm sorry," Dire said, sounding as if he genuinely meant it. He pressed slight fingers to his breastbone, as if trying to soothe an aching spot on his chest. "But I can't talk about Tynne's bargain."

"Could you talk about it with Winnie, since she's part of it?"

"No. It was made by your mother, so I can only speak of it with your mother—"

"My ma is gone!"

"I'm bound by this rule. I'm no freer than any of you." He turned a bit, shadows falling over his face, hiding away the magic of his clouded eye. He murmured, "I know it's a funeral, and funerals are a sad business, but I miss seeing people. The Parletts used to visit my home for the holidays. They stopped coming years ago. Sometimes, I miss that."

Eliza drew back. The Serlings spent holidays with neighbors and friends. What would it be like to spend them with… no one?

Dire patted the pockets of his jacket and pulled out a long feather, gray streaking through the white. He passed it to her. "I found this on my way here and thought Winnie might like it."

Eliza stared at the feather in horror. She didn't take it, and after a pause, Dire set it on one of Pa's barrels.

"You know your birthday is the when," he said. "You know your mother is the who. All you need is the what—the why. Find those."

"I'll be able to save Winnie, then?" When was it that Eliza had decided to trust him?

"Maybe. Hopefully. Hopefully, you'll be able to save yourself too."

Sweat dripped down Eliza's hairline. She couldn't breathe. *She didn't have to.*

One, two, three. Save Winnie.

Four, five, six. Save herself.

Seven, eight, nine. "How?" she asked. "How am I supposed to find out the what and the why?"

A commotion outside drew Dire's attention—the screech of a bird of prey.

"I don't know." Dire turned and headed for the door. "But Eliza, I suggest you hurry."

EIGHTEEN

*Filemon Hardwick dreamed. He made shadow
puppets against Cape Fen's shifting, ghostly fog that
turned real as soon as he dropped his hands. They
waved and he waved back, watching as they floated
into the sky. He missed them, even though they
weren't real. But he didn't need to dream and wish
for friends; he had a true friend of his own: Eliza.*

E liza left the workroom in a daze. She felt the seams along
her insides popping, a large piece of her falling out of place.
She struggled to hold herself together.

Today was Monday. Wednesday was her birthday. Only two days stretched between now and the end of Ma's bargain.

Winnie streaked through the yard, chasing after Filemon. Her mouth dropped open and she screamed, except it wasn't the scream of a little girl; it was the scream of a bird. The screech Eliza had heard moments before.

"*Winnie!*" she shouted, and Win stopped. "When did you start doing that—that sound?"

"Today? Yesterday? I don't remember." Winnie smiled. "It's good, isn't it?"

She crossed to her sister and smoothed her hands down Win's hair, a feather shaking loose from the strands. She met Filemon's gaze. "It's very good. It sounds quite real."

"What are you thinking?" Filemon asked.

Eliza covered Winnie's ears, but her sister squirmed away and ducked out of reach.

"Tell me too," she said. "You can't just tell Filemon and keep me out."

"The Parletts aren't here," Eliza said. "None of them arrived after the funeral."

"Maybe they're late."

"I don't think so. If they're not here yet, I don't think they're coming. I've done everything else I can think to fix things, except for talking with them."

"*Shh.*" Filemon waved Eliza to be silent, nodding to where his dad hovered at the back of the Jester. Filemon waved to him, a forced grin pasted to his face. "Ten minutes. Ten minutes now. He checks on me every ten minutes."

Basil Hardwick nodded at them, and then disappeared inside.

Filemon turned and said in desperation, "Whatever you have planned, count me in."

Eliza did indeed have a plan, one she'd held in her mind since Colby first crouched beside her at school and asked about the Wolf. Ma's family understood more about Dire's magic and how bargains worked than anyone, but she'd always been told to stay far, far away from them. It was time to give in and ask them what they knew.

"I'm going to get Zilpha to take me to the Parletts," Eliza said.

"Us. Zilpha's going to take *us* to the Parletts." Winnie's frown twisted. "Why are we going to Ma's family? Pa doesn't allow us there."

"Because they know more about Dire's magic than anyone. They've met with Dire and his Wolf before. Colby said it's like a rite of passage. Dire won't tell details about Ma's bargain, and Pa knows nothing, but the Parletts might," she said. "So we go to the Parletts, we learn about Ma and about what she would've bargained for, and we use that to keep you safe."

"Pa will be mad."

"We won't tell him. He won't even notice we're gone."

～

Miniscule flakes of snow floated through the crisp air, as chill and frozen as the silence that descended on Old Queen Mae Street. Zilpha wasn't inside. She wasn't outside. She wasn't anywhere.

"Doggone it! Where is she?" Eliza said in frustration.

"Don't say bad words, Liza," Winnie said, sounding enough like Pa that heat rose in Eliza's cheeks.

The trio walked down the street, shouting her name, and there she appeared from between two houses.

Barefoot as always, Zilpha folded her arms and said, "What trouble are you getting into now?"

"We're going to your old home, where the Parletts live," Winnie said.

"Are you now?" Zilpha said.

"And you're going to take us," Eliza said.

"Am I?"

Winnie scratched her head. More feathers fell from the scruff to tumble down and decorate her gray funeral clothes.

But for a tic beneath her right eye, Zilpha stayed expressionless. She watched Winnie, gaze locking on the smattering of down. "Your ma would be furious if she were here and knew I was going to take you to the place she'd left."

"She's not here. She disappeared. Besides, if you don't take us, we'll find someone else who will," Eliza said. "Mr. Hardwick or Mr. Chess or…Sheriff Olavi. Or, or we'll call Lionel. He'd come pick us up."

"And I'd tell your pa, and he'd refused to let you go anywhere." Zilpha rubbed her brow. "Why does this matter so much? What do you hope to gain by going there?"

Desperate hope grew in Eliza. "I need to understand Dire's magic. They're the only ones who seem to know."

Zilpha eyes fluttered shut. "Lionel. If you want to know how the bargains work, you'll have to speak with Lionel. Of all of us, he understands the most."

"Even more than you?"

"I never spoke much with Dire about his magic." Zilpha strode toward her motorcar. "Eliza, my family may not tell you the answers you hope to hear."

"But maybe they'll know what Ma bargained for."

"*I* know what your ma bargained for. If you thought on it hard enough, you'd know too. She bargained for *you*."

"I know that part!"

Her aunt paused, face angling in her direction, though not quite making eye contact. "Eliza, I don't quite think you do."

~

As they drove, Eliza pulled this truth from Zilpha: Tynne wanted children. She and Waylon couldn't have children, and so she bargained with Dire for help.

Quiet filled the motorcar. Filemon sat beside the passenger side door, with Winnie at his left, Eliza to her left, and Zilpha driving—all of them squashed and uncomfortable in the silence as Zilpha took them out of town.

"Pa knew?" Eliza asked. He hadn't mentioned this the night before.

"He knew," Zilpha said, "but I don't think he understood."

Eliza didn't quite understand either. If Ma bargained to get daughters, then Mrs. Chess had been telling the truth—Ma hadn't bargained to get off the Cape. Why then had she disappeared and where had she disappeared to?

They drove off Old Queen Mae and took side roads, crossing to the southern edge of the Cape where a twenty-seven acre stretch of land belonged to the Parletts. They were one of the oldest families on the Cape, going back well before Dire's grandmother ever fell in love with Fen. In fact, the Parlett name was half the reason many visited the Cape to begin with.

Beaches. Ocean. Whale-watching. Ice cream. Fancy parties…and, the Parletts.

Ma's family's land butted up against the ocean on the Cape's southern side and called one of the most idyllic beaches its own. Rumors galore surrounded that beach. It was off limits to visitors, though it could be easily accessed by the ocean. Some said skeletons danced beneath the waves. Others claimed the sand gave off toxic fumes. Still others said that a horrendous riptide dragged down anyone who didn't bleed Parlett blood.

They turned onto a gravel road and passed beneath a canopy of long-fingered trees, their bare limbs skewering the gray sky. Snowflakes fell and spattered against the windshield. Eliza clutched Winnie's hand, forcing herself not to squeeze too tight with nervousness.

Zilpha parked the motorcar at an iron gate barricading the road. Twisted lettering read: THE PARLETTS', WHERE DREAMS ROAR. Zilpha got out and unhooked the latch to the gate. Iron hinges protested, squealing against the cold.

Eliza shuddered as they drove onto the Parlett lands. She looked out at the sky—they were still far from night, but she checked and triple checked for the moon's presence. She didn't want to be out when the Wolf appeared. They dropped down a small hill and entered the property, where haphazard buildings scattered and land, all different shapes and heights and each with their own signage. THE HUNTRESS, read one. THE BADGER, read another. THE WEREWOLF, THE HYENA,

The Viper, The Elephant, The Poison Dart Frog, The Arctic Fox... All cabins that would be full of tourists come summer.

They were marks of Parletts gone by. A circus of sorts. Real circuses often visited during summer, though they rarely stayed for long. Years ago, the Little Sister's circus came to visit, though when they left, their most famous contortionist stayed past First Frost. She'd married Mr. Gorham, bargained with Dire, and now predicted weather patterns for the Cape's inhabitants—including the terrible storm from several nights before. She always said she knew when bad weather was coming because she felt as if she were made of birds and animals trying to flee the coast.

Zilpha drove down a small side road that took them past one cozy house and then another, eventually parking before a cottage-style home. Strands of green tinsel wrapped around the white bannisters of the front porch and two stuffed snowmen sat on the rocking chairs out front.

All four climbed from the motorcar into the crisp day, the quiet only broken by a steady *thump-thump* coming from the side of the house. Curiosity piqued, Eliza stepped to the side and peered around the corner. Lionel Parlett's son chopped wood through an iron wood splitter. Her cousin didn't stop hammering logs through the splitter, though he did look up and wink at her.

She didn't bother saying hello. Her cousin had always been strange, just like his father, although his hair was jet black, not dyed some changing shade of brown, gray, or white.

Zilpha stomped up the porch and rapped hard on the door. It opened, revealing Eliza's uncle. Her nostrils flared; Lionel smelled of cranberry tea and anger. The combination upset her already tense stomach.

"Lionel," Zilpha blew on her hands again, not quite meeting her brother's gaze.

"Hello, sister." Lionel leaned against the door frame. "I haven't seen you in ages—you even managed to skip the First Frost gathering. I was starting to think you were avoiding me."

"You'd be right about that." Zilpha turned and gestured to Eliza. "Ask your questions."

"I adore questions. I know answers to many things," Lionel said.

"Make sure you give the right answers."

"Clever to demand that, considering the right answer isn't always the most truthful answer." A sneaky smile glinted in Lionel's eyes. "Why don't you come in, where we can talk out of the cold? I can make tea."

"We need to know about the bargains," Eliza said, not agreeing to go in. "We need to know how to stop the bargain around Winnie, how to make Winnie stop changing. I need to understand Dire's magic." Too much tumbled loose inside her, and she didn't know where to start so she started with it all.

Lionel reached inside for a coat and draped it over his shoulders to block the cold. "Where do you think the Wolf goes when it's day?"

Taken aback at the change in topic, Eliza leaned back. "I assume it sleeps somewhere."

"In Dire's house?"

"No." She'd been to Dire's house. There hadn't been a wolf curled before the fire or on the kitchen floor. "It probably sleeps in a cave or something. Or, I don't know, maybe Dire gave it a house and it sleeps in a bed."

"Rumors have gotten in the way of truth for a long while now, but every year, we tell the Wolf's origin story and because of it, we know the root of Dire's magic. Eliza, in that story, what's the only thing the magic does?"

Eliza held tight to Winnie's hand, feeling as if she were in school and Miss Alayna had asked her a particularly difficult question. A baron had fallen in love with Dire's grandmother, and he said he'd do anything to be with her. "She turned a man into a wolf."

"Shape-shifting is a very old form of magic. You've likely heard of werewolves—they're only one sort of shape-shifter though. Our Dire Witches are another sort." Lionel stared straight at Eliza. "We know Dire's magic can change people into animals from the origin story, but sometimes, I wonder if he can do the opposite."

"He could turn the Wolf back human?"

"Yes, though that's not what I was getting at."

"But why does it matter if Dire turns the baron back human? He'd be over a hundred years old!"

Lionel looked stricken. "You think the Wolf *then* is the Wolf *now*? The first Dire Witch died, just as her first wolf died."

Eliza pulled Winnie behind her. She felt like a trap had settled over her without her knowing, and she needed to find a way to escape. "What does *any* of this have to do with the bargain around Winnie?"

"Because it has to do with your mother's bargain."

"I don't understand!"

"It's one and the same, Eliza. Your mother's bargain *is* Winnie's bargain. The only way to end what's happening to Winnie is to end what's happening to your Ma."

"Ma's gone!"

"No. She *disappeared*. Disappearing isn't the same as being gone."

"Ma couldn't have children, so she made a bargain to get Winnie and me, and…and now Winnie has a bargain, and…"

Eliza has assumed there were two bargains: the one Ma made

years ago to be able to have Eliza and Winnie, and the one that now made feathers fall from Winnie's head. But what if they were the same? She dragged her gaze up to Lionel and murmured, "Ma's bargain and Winnie's bargain are one bargain. Not two."

"Do you know what Dire wants most in the entire world?" Lionel asked.

"*Friendship*," Zilpha murmured from where she leaned against the porch railing.

"But no one's willing to be friends with the scary witch who lives next door. He's not entirely powerless though, is he? So, how then does he get friends?"

"He has no friends," Eliza said.

"You're right. He doesn't. And so instead, he *makes* them, and he makes them by bargaining."

Snow fell in soft patterns outside the porch, melting quick on the ground. Her world shifted. "Oh. *Oh*," she said.

Her thoughts came slow, but when they landed, they planted inside her, roots burrowing through her limbs. The first witch changed a man into a magical wolf because of his dream of love. Had Dire changed people into magical wolves for the sake of friendship? Was this where Mr. Chess had disappeared when he'd bargained for Mrs. Chess? Was this where *Ma* had disappeared when she'd bargained for Winnie and Eliza?

She held tighter to Win's hand. "Is Ma...the Wolf?"

Lionel shrugged one shoulder, as if the answer didn't matter. "That would be my assumption, yes."

Wonder unfurled inside her.

"You have your answers, Eliza. We need to go," Zilpha said from behind them.

"I'm sorry, sister." Lionel's face creased. "Know how sorry I am, but I really can't let you go."

NINETEEN

—

Lionel Parlett dreamed. He stood in a wintry tundra,
right beside a pure white arctic fox. He blended in
here, all the pieces of him—white hair and white
clothes and white hard-soled boots—camouflaging
him against the snow that flurried about. When they
were young, Tynne and Zilpha used to stand here
beside him, dreaming of impossible things. But then
they'd gone, and he was left alone to weather the storm.

M*a, the Wolf. Ma, the Wolf. Ma, the Wolf.* Because of course,
in the strange way the Cape worked, this made sense.

Dire kept to tradition, and the tradition had always been to have wolves, so why wouldn't he have turned Ma into a wolf? Into *the* Wolf?

But would it end? Would Ma ever come back? Would Winnie ever be safe?

Winnie screamed.

Eliza whirled at the same time she heard a heavy thump. She pushed Winnie toward Zilpha's motorcar, looking for what had scared her sister. She froze, because their mother wasn't standing behind them in wolf form. Instead, it was Loretta Parlett, whose husband's funeral had just taken place. She crouched above Zilpha, one hand gloved and the other bare with palm pressed to Zilpha's neck. Zilpha lay in the snow, chest rising and falling with quiet breath, and eyes closed in sleep.

Loretta smelled of an iron-tang, except the scent was sharper. More toxic. It reminded Eliza of the blue octopus that had washed up on Cape Fen when she was little and that Ma had refused to let her go near.

Stay far away, said Ma's voice in her ears, and Eliza obeyed. She pressed Winnie against her back, her sister digging fingers into the thin fabric of her shirt. She took one step and then another, until she stood shoulder-to-shoulder with Filemon.

"She's only sleeping," Loretta said, a soft frown tugging at her lips as she watched Zilpha sleep.

"I want to go home," Winnie said.

Lionel tsked. "You are home, littlings. Your mother merely kidnapped you away." He switched places with Loretta and hefted Zilpha into his arms. "All I need is for your mother's bargain to end and for you to change. Once that happens and once Tynne comes back from her stint as Wolf, she'll understand that you all belong here. We're Parletts. We were never meant to be apart—we're family and nothing's more important than family."

"I don't want you as family," Eliza said.

"Thank goodness you have no choice," Lionel said, sadness etching through his features. He turned away with Zilpha cradled to his chest.

Eliza kept her gaze locked on Loretta's hands as she ushered them inside.

A crackling fire inside a hearth in the living room to their left enveloped them in warmth. Dark, wood flooring shone, as if it'd recently been sponged clean, and on top of it lay a large rug with an intricate design. Tassels at the ends stretched out straight. Eliza couldn't help but imagine that if this same rug were placed in the Fen Jester that Winnie would braid the tassels together.

Loretta directed them toward a set of high-backed chairs by the fire, and Eliza was careful to muss up the edges of the rug, at least to make the cabin look more lived in than what it did. Everything from the positions of the chairs to the book set at a perfect right angle on a table to a glass bowl containing what looked to be collectors' marbles, the entire house looked fake. It was as if it were staged to impress visitors.

Eliza wasn't impressed.

Loretta made tea and handed out popcorn dusted in cinnamon sugar. And in all that time, she kept one hand gloved and the other bare, and Eliza kept Winnie well away from both.

"You can't keep us here forever," Eliza said, edging her voice with the iron she didn't actually feel. "It's not like Pa won't be able to find us—Cape Fen isn't that big."

Loretta leaned one hip against an empty chair, but then pushed away and strode to the front door. "You remind me of Tynne. Hopeful and protective and…dreamy." She pulled on her second glove. "Lionel doesn't need to keep you here forever. He says we just need to keep you here until it turns night. The Wolf will come and when it does—"

"Ma. You mean Ma." Eliza gripped a teacup tight between her hands. She should chuck it at Loretta's head. If she knocked her unconscious, they could escape out the door.

Loretta adjusted the fingers to her glove. "I suppose so, yes, though Tynne doesn't realize it." She turned the handle of the door, but paused and looked back, meeting Eliza's gaze, and for a moment—for the time it took Eliza to close her lungs to air—it felt as if she cared. "Sometimes, family feels fragile, but blood isn't something that can be broken. All we've ever dreamed of is having all the Parletts together again on one plot of land, bargaining with Dire's magic just as we have for the last hundred years. Tynne and Zilpha's leaving was very painful for both Lionel and me. You belong in this family, Eliza." She left then, closing and locking the door behind her.

"Kendare just died," Filemon said. "Why is she so concerned with you and Winnie?"

"Maybe that's why. Maybe she's scared of losing more people," Eliza said, though understanding her aunt and uncle was not at the top of her priority list. It was time to escape. She leapt out of her seat and ran to the door, pulling on the handle and saying, "If Ma is the Wolf, why did she try to attack us?"

"She didn't," Winnie grumbled. "I already told you. She was trying to say *hello*."

"No! No, the Wolf…it jumped for us with teeth bared. I know it did. I was there!"

"I was there too!"

"Can we talk about that later?" Filemon said. "Right now, I want to get out of here."

Eliza and Winnie agreed, and they all dispersed in separate directions, trying find a way out. Eliza turned her back to Winnie and Filemon and spread open her hands, glaring at her knuckles. They'd hurt for days, but it had gotten worse, and the bones had all throbbed when she'd pulled on the door just now. She massaged the joints, hoping for relief, but—

"Eliza, come help," said Winnie.

One, two, three. She rubbed her hands once more and told herself to forget the pain.

Twenty-eight, twenty-nine, thirty. Eliza, Winnie, and Filemon tested the windows.

Fifty-five, fifty-six, fifty-seven. They tested the door.

One hundred and sixty-two, one hundred and sixty-three, one hundred and sixty-four. They banged and pried at every exit they could find, but the house was too sturdy and the glass of the windows was too thick, and soon they wore themselves tired.

Two hundred and twelve, two hundred and thirteen, two hundred and fourteen. Outside, snow continued to fall and the sun continued to set, bringing them closer to night. Closer to the Wolf. Closer to the end.

Two hundred and ninety-eight, two hundred and ninety-nine, three hundred. "Are you guys coming, or what?" Solid and real, Colby stood in a stairwell at the back of the kitchen opposite the living room. She held open a door that had blocked the stairwell and had been locked a moment before. Paper-thin spiderwebbed lace covered her from head-to-toe, like the decoration on one of Mrs. Landis's ornamental cakes.

Eliza's heart hammered in her chest. Her limbs felt as if they were on fire. "What are you doing?"

"Saving you, duh. Auntie Tynne kept you away from here to keep you safe, to make it so that you'd have a choice over bargaining or not. Parletts don't have a choice when they live on Parlett lands. Don't know why you came back, especially now." Colby gestured them to follow her upstairs, and after the slightest hesitation, they did.

"Is Zilpha okay?" Winnie asked as they climbed past the second floor and to the third.

Eliza started. She'd been so consumed with getting Winnie out, she'd forgotten about their aunt.

"She's just sleeping. Lionel laid her in her motorcar. Unless she's hunting, Auntie Loretta doesn't often poison to kill," Colby said.

"Hunting… Poison to kill?" Filemon asked from behind Eliza.

"Sure. She bargained to always be able to protect herself—you remember her awful first husband. Now she has poison-skin. Dire took inspiration from some sort of poisonous frog. Although, in my opinion, it's a shoddy thing to have gotten. She'll never be able to touch anyone again without hurting them, not that she wants to." Colby stopped after the second flight of stairs and entered an open doorway. "Windows are unlocked on the third floor. The adults get pretty nervous come tourist season and think people will break in, so they bar windows up to the second floor."

"We're going to climb out a *third-story* window?" Eliza asked.

"I climbed up but climbing down is always harder." Colby shrugged. "Besides, I told you, all Parletts are good at sneaking. The Wolf'll be here soon. I assume you want to be long gone by then."

"But the Wolf is Ma," Winnie said.

"It *was* your ma. It doesn't much matter what the Wolf was, only what it is, and right now, it's Dire's servant."

Colby told Filemon where to find rope, and he disappeared, clomping back down the steps. When he reappeared, it was with a long rope in hand. He set to rigging up a levy system, tying a looped sling around Winnie.

Colby bit her lips together. At last, she said, "Don't blame Dire."

"I can blame him plenty," Eliza said.

"It's not his fault things are the way they are. He was born into this bargaining system just like we were," Colby said. "The Parletts are the only ones on this dumb island to seek Dire out for anything other than bargain-making. Sometimes he comes over and plays cards with us, but Lionel and Loretta are never very nice. They always try to convince him to stay during summer and perform at the circus. Obviously, he refuses. He always seems sad. It got worse after your mom bargained and he lost Zilpha."

"How did he *lose* her because of my ma?"

Colby said, "The way my dad tells it is that Tynne bargained and disappeared, and then Zilpha bargained to have some sort of ability to keep an eye on you and Winnie. She wanted to keep you two safe. Dire saw it as a betrayal, that she used him for his magic."

"She didn't use him! He should've helped her because they were friends," Eliza said. "Are you telling me I should feel bad for Dire because he's made mistakes, is sad, and no one's nice to him anymore? Because I don't."

"No. I think he'd be mad if you pitied him."

"I don't pity him. He turns people into wolves so he can have friends. That's *not* a good way to make friends." She spoke to Colby, though she watched Winnie as she sat on the edge of the window and tested Filemon's sling. "And it's not a good way to honor the magic his grandmother did."

"You mean the wolf-making? I told you not to listen to Jarvis Bodfish's origin story of Dire. I told you he leaves out all the good stuff." Colby took hold of the rope Filemon passed her, and spoke, voice dropping into words worn smooth by a story she'd clearly told before: "Once there was a moon witch, a dreaming witch, a *dire* witch who landed on Cape Fen's shores. Her heart ached at Fen's wintry beauty, and so she decided to stay. She fell in love with a human, but the difference between witch and human was too great, and she knew he would never understand her magic. Dire was a witch who could use the magic of the *moon*, though, and so when sun's magic-killing rays disappeared and the moon rose, she crept into the dreams of the baron and read his heart's greatest desire: *to be loved by Dire completely*. And so, out of the magic of the moon, she wove a spell. Of the baron's skin, she made a fur cloak. Of his teeth, she made fangs. Of his hands, she made claws. Of his body, she made a wolf. It was the fiercest spell she'd ever made, and she understood the unbalanced nature of it: more magic than man, which meant he wouldn't ever be able to exist during the day. It didn't matter. It gave her a companion, and it fulfilled his deepest wish. Like this, the dire witch would love him forever."

The story floated around in Eliza's head. Parts felt similar to Mr. Bodfish's story: a witch, a baron, a wolf. But the differences were sharp and sweet, and Eliza picked them out. In Mr. Bodfish's story, the man loved the witch, and because of it, she turned him into a wolf and stole his title. It was *his* dream and *his* love that transformed him. But in Colby's story, the witch loved the man and he loved her. She sought a solution for the mess they were in, and it was his dream that fulfilled both their wishes. It wasn't a one-sided story of one-sided love; nor was it a story wrapped in elegant beginnings and neat endings. It was magical and messy and felt closer to the truth.

"I don't know what any of that matters," she admitted.

"Nothing, probably." Colby grinned, lopsided and secretive. "Listen, Dire's magic is moon and dreaming magic. He listens to people's dreams, but the only way to make those dreams come true is with his shape-shifting magic, because moon magic *is* shape-shifting magic. A person might dream of hearing the best gossip, and they end up with animal ears. A person could dream of predicting weather, and they end up with the animal instinct to run when storms roll in. Or maybe somebody dreams of a warning system to know when their father is around, and they get a snake's heat-sensing eyes. That's what I have, you know?"

Eliza's mouth parted. "*You?*"

"Of course. I had to dream for something, so I dreamed to be able to know where people were—my dad and siblings. In the end, I can sort of see through walls; I can track people. It's not the best gift, but it's also not the worst." Colby shrugged. "This is what people don't understand. The bargains aren't actual bargains. They aren't *if you give me* this, *I'll give you* that *in return.*

At least, they weren't. Your mother was the first person to have ever done that. Your mom's bargain was what gave Bri Hardwick inspiration for his."

"Then what have all the other bargains been?"

"Since the very first bargain that was made between the first witch and our great-grandparents, bargains have only been wishes that the Dires have made come true. That's it. As long as we agreed to stay trapped on Cape Fen and supply the Dires with magic, they would make our dreams real. Except the witch we have now has always been so bad at what he does, there have been strange consequences. It didn't used to be like this."

"I don't dream," Eliza said.

"Are you sure?"

Eliza held Colby's gaze, strangely positive that her cousin understood her better than anyone else. She didn't like it.

"I'll tell you this, Eliza. Dire isn't like his mother or grandmother. He never really wanted the magic, and because of that, the magic controls him more than he controls the magic."

"How is my knowing that supposed to help anything?"

"Dunno," Colby said with a grin. "But the information might come in handy later."

Winnie sat back in the swing Filemon had made and slowly, they lowered her down. She walked her feet along the side of the house, laughing and whispering to herself.

Eliza didn't laugh with her sister. Relief didn't loosen the muscles in her back. She was pulled taut with fear. She narrowed her eyes and looked across the Parlett grounds, spying through the evening for evidence that Lionel or Loretta had returned. She didn't spot her uncle's odd hair or her aunt's gloved hands; instead, the eyes of the Wolf glowed back at her.

"Up, up, *up!*" she screamed. Breath jammed in her throat. Her pulse skittered high. "Pull Winnie up!"

She snatched up Winnie's rope, pulling hard enough to strain the muscles in her arms and back. The rope snagged. She shouted. She looked over the edge to see that it wasn't the rope that had snagged, but that Winnie had gripped the upper lip of the second-floor window with two hands and had braced her feet on the bottom, making it impossible for Eliza and Colby and Filemon to haul her up.

"*Momma?*" Winnie shouted down to the Wolf.

"That's not Ma right now, Winnie." Eliza pulled harder at the rope.

"*STOP!*" Winnie shouted.

Evening shadows fell over the grounds, the sun's power fading to give way to the moon's magic. By what little light was left, Eliza saw the Wolf hadn't moved. It sat on its haunches, docile and sweet. It shifted, and Eliza flinched, but all it did was lift its snout, part its jaws, and howl. The warbling pitch began low and soared up, stretching across the night and eating up the distance between them.

"*Oh.*" The soft word tumbled from Winnie. "That's…the sound. It's like flying."

Eliza strained to listen, but in the Wolf's howl, she didn't hear the beat of wings against air; she heard the swish of fins against water. In the Wolf's howl, soft bubbles burst against her fiery skin. In the Wolf's howl, the dark of the ocean clamped down on the anxiety that chafed at her insides.

No.

One, two, three. Eliza had too much to do, too much to keep safe.

Four, five, six. She couldn't listen to the Wolf that was once her mother.

Seven, eight, nine. She faced the beast. She sucked in air until her lungs strained, and she shouted, "NO!"

"*Yes,*" Winnie whispered.

Eliza's heart plummeted. She looked down at Winnie, the Wolf forgotten. Winnie's gaze locked on the stars far above, on the place where the Wolf's howl gathered in the dark, and as Eliza watched, her eyes changed. Her pupils widened, spread out and encompassed the white. Her face flattened, nose hooking outward and deepening in color. The smallest feathery hairs sprouted from her cheekbones and forehead.

"Please, please, *no*," Eliza moaned. "No, no, Winnie." She stretched down, trying to reach for the downy plumes that decorated Winnie's skin, but she was too far away.

The Wolf's howl died, and in its place, Winnie shrieked. The high-pitched sound delved straight into Eliza's skull, sending her ears ringing and shattering the *hush-hush* of the night. The Wolf's nose lifted. Its jaws came unhinged. Another howl flew from its throat to join the echoes of Winnie's cry.

"She's an owl," Filemon said, awe filling his voice.

"Stop, stop, stop." In desperation, Eliza pulled and pulled at the rope, but Winnie had gotten herself wedged just right. "Stop, Winnie. Make it stop."

Winnie's gaze stayed locked on the sky, and her ears stayed tuned to the Wolf's song.

"Pull her up, Filemon," Eliza shouted.

"It's too late," Colby said. "She'll still be able to hear the sound from inside the house."

"It can't be too late!" Eliza leaned as far forward as she could. Colby grabbed the back of her shirt to keep her from tumbling out the window. She reached for Winnie, but she came up short.

The Wolf's howl started up again. The eerie sound zipped through her, and her heart fluttered faster. From below, claws scrabbled against wood. Another owl screech left her sister's mouth.

From very far away, a truck door slammed. "Eliza! Winnie!" shouted Pa, voice cracking the louder it got.

A second door slammed, and a second voice shouted: "Filemon!" Mr. Hardwick had arrived to find his son.

Eliza couldn't care about that. All that mattered was that below her, her sister turned her head too far past her shoulders, looking behind her in the Wolf's direction. With a rush of movement, Winnie kicked off her boots and socks. She hooked clawed toes into the side of the house and climbed, scrambling past the third story window and onto the roof.

"Help me." Eliza placed her feet on the windowsill and turned with hands reaching for the gutter along the roof.

"Eliza!" Filemon shouted. He grabbed onto her waist, but Eliza stepped up, kicking him in the shoulder and then finding the hands he offered up, standing as he pushed. She pulled hard against the edge of the roof to lift herself onto the shingles.

Filemon pushed and she pulled, and fear scraped through her body. She clawed her way up, digging her boots into the edge of the gutter, and climbed until she reached the angled roof on which Winnie perched. Feathers adorned her hair, her face, her arms, neck, and back, poking free of her coat. Her fingers spread wide, catching updrafts of air and tracking small shifts of wind. She clacked her teeth—her *beak*—and let loose a shriek. It pierced the night, cutting wide the white, full moon over head.

"Please, Winnie." Eliza inched toward her sister. "*Win*. Come down. You only need to wait until my birthday and then everything will be better. You have a choice in this. Please."

Winnie's head twisted, her shoulders moving not the slightest, as if she heard something in the distance, as if she listened to the scampering of miniature claws against the earth, as if far away, a mouse scrabbled against the damp bark of a tree in search of nuts and wintertime food.

"Winnie. *You have a choice*."

And she did. Winnie did have a choice, and it was *her* choice. Hers alone.

Which was probably why she jumped.

TWENTY

—

Loretta Parlett dreamed. She dreamed and
dreamed and dreamed of protection, of a way to
keep herself safe from anyone who might ever
do her harm. She held a tiny golden dart frog in
her hand and drew its poison into her skin.

One, two, three. Despair threaded through Eliza's limbs. Seeped into the fibers of her muscles, her ligaments, her bones. Drew into the backs of her eyes and the roof of her mouth and—

"Eliza?" From behind her on the roof, Pa's soft voice floated into the sky.

"Winnie's gone." Eliza tracked Winnie's monstrous shadow as she swooped low over Eliza's head. Pa crouched on the roof behind her, and now, finally, all of her fury poured free. "You said there wasn't anything to worry about. You said everything would be fine!"

Pa raised his arms, but then they fell to his side, limp. Like this, he reminded Eliza of the weeks after their mother disappeared. Hopeless.

"Ma made a bargain with Dire to have Winnie and me!" Eliza shouted. "She couldn't have babies."

"I know."

"How could you know and not tell me? You didn't think it important to ask where I came from?"

"When your mother arrived home with you, I didn't ask what she'd done. I couldn't admit that she'd bargained with Dire without me. She didn't speak of it. She knew my family loathed Dire's magic, and I never asked. And...she wasn't the only one who wanted children. I wanted—*needed*—you to exist too."

Eliza understood this: her mother loved her and Winnie enough to bargain for them, and Pa loved all three enough not to ask questions.

"I've worked so hard on your ma's sleeping draught, and sometimes...I've wondered if I could give it to Dire. If it would quiet his magic and stop his dreams. If that's how I could get him to tell me what had happened to Tynne."

"Why haven't you used it?"

Pa lifted his arms again, shrugging twice before letting them drop back to his side.

"You could've brought it to his house or given it to him at the Jester! He was *there*. He likes playing card games. He would've sat with you."

"And trapped me in a bargain, while he was at it!"

"No." Eliza remembered the game she'd played with Dire. He might've twisted her words, but he'd never tried to make her bargain; he'd almost seemed as if he didn't want her to. She watched her pa and realization dawned. "You were scared."

"I knew the sleeping draught worked on people, but I didn't know if it'd work on him. I couldn't afford to get it wrong and waste the only opportunity I'd get."

"You should've listened to the Parletts in that, Pa. Dire would've had you back. He would've asked for another game." She pointed at the sky. "Now it doesn't matter. Winnie's already gone."

Pa shoved one fist against his mouth. She didn't need to ask if he had anything else to tell, because it was clear how little he knew. He'd never had the courage to ask the questions that needed to be asked.

"Dire said Ma's bargain ends on my birthday which means that whatever's happening with Winnie will end then too. What if she doesn't turn human before that? What if she's stuck a bird *forever*?" Eliza said.

The bargain their mother struck would end just days away. Eliza wouldn't be rash. She would stay calm, and she would save Winnie.

"Winnie will have to save herself," Pa said, and Eliza realized she'd spoken her thoughts aloud. "It's her choice. It's her bargain to play out."

"No." Eliza crawled toward the edge of the roof. "It's not her bargain; it's *Ma's* bargain. Winnie had no choice in whether or not she played. If she has any say in what happens next, I will give her the best chance possible. I can do it. I can make a bargain that will save her."

"No!" Pa gripped her shoulder before she could swing off the edge of the roof. "You're not allowed."

Eliza peered up at his face. "You're not so unlike them, you know?"

Pa's fingers tightened.

"The Serlings and the Parletts *both* want to control Dire's bargains. The Serlings want them to go away, and the Parletts want to use them. But you can't control the magic. You can't! Ma knew that."

A wave of silence and stillness seeped out of Eliza to blanket the night, and Pa didn't speak into it. He let go of her shoulder. She swung off the roof, feet flailing as she searched for the windowsill. Instead, large hands gripped her and pulled her inside. Mr. Hardwick.

"Hello," she said and darted out from beneath his grasp, running fast enough to trip and tumble down the stairs. She rolled to her feet, bruises forming on her hips and knees, and fled from the house, barely noticing the splintered front door as she ran into the night.

"Filemon! *Filemon!*" she screamed.

"I'm here." Filemon stood beside Zilpha's motorcar. "We're going somewhere else, aren't we?"

"You're not going anywhere," Lionel said from behind them. "I won't allow my family to keep abandoning me. The Parletts are all supposed to stay together."

"And no one's ever supposed to move away?" Filemon asked. "That makes *no* sense! You can't trap someone for all eternity. It doesn't work like that."

"You're right," Mr. Hardwick said from behind Eliza. "And I'm sorry I've done it to you, Filemon. At some point, Lionel, you'll have to find a way to let go."

"Letting go is giving up," Lionel said.

Mr. Hardwick barked out a laugh. "Letting go is saying it's okay not to be in control, and now, I suggest you get out of our way."

The Wolf howled again and chaos erupted: a crack resounded behind them, blowing out Eliza's hearing. Pa tackled her. The ground flew out from beneath her feet. They landed with a *whoomp*, and her breath squashed out of her lungs. She whimpered and worked her jaws. Sound popped back—

"Stop shooting! *Olavi!* Stop!" Mr. Hardwick screamed.

Except Sheriff Olavi didn't pause. She ran with her rifle in one hand, heading down the gravel road in the direction the loping Wolf escaped.

"Let her kill it," Pa growled as he pulled Eliza to her feet.

"It's not a wolf, Pa; it's *Ma!*"

Pa's face shifted, micro expressions crossing his skin like runes for Eliza to read. "It's not. It can't be. She...she can't be."

"Ma turned into the Wolf for Winnie and me, just like Mr. Chess turned into the Wolf for Mrs. Chess. Turning into the Wolf is payment when you bargain *for* someone. It's the price Dire takes," Eliza said. "The Wolf doesn't kill people. The Wolf is just... It's Dire's friend. *Ma is the Wolf!*"

Pa took a last look at her. He spun toward Mr. Hardwick, said, "Take care of her," and then he ran. His footsteps crunched against gravel, taking him down the moonlit road, and Eliza's legs stopped working. Her knees quivered. A hand appeared and she clasped it, grateful for Filemon's strength.

Eliza watched Pa run, chasing after Sheriff Olavi...and

Ma. She turned back toward Mr. Hardwick, and instead found Lionel standing in her way.

"I'm not letting you leave." Lionel blocked her path.

"Really, Dad?" Colby Parlett said from where she stood on the front porch.

The two-toned hair atop Lionel's head bobbed as he jerked in her direction.

"You have to let them go. You have to let *all* of this go." Colby took a step forward, hands on her hips.

"No!" Lionel said, sounding sad and angry and confused, and in his distraction, Filemon helped Eliza into the motorcar, pushing the sleeping Zilpha over to make room. Mr. Hardwick fit the crank into the engine and turned it with one hard push.

"Nothing is as it was when Grandma was alive, Dad." Colby folded her arms. "It has to be okay that the family moves out and that things change."

"No!" Lionel shouted. He made one last attempt to stop them, but Mr. Hardwick spurred the motorcar and bumped Lionel's side, making him tumble to the ground.

As they drove away, Eliza looked back at the place she might've grown up, had Ma kept them more Parlett than Serling, and saw Colby's silhouette standing in the road beside her father, one hand lifted in a wave. She thought she understood; Colby wanted to escape and live life a different way than her father envisioned.

Eliza waved back and then focused. She had a game to win against Dire.

TWENTY-ONE

—

Colby Parlett dreamed. There, her father
asked, "What do you dream for?" and she
was brave enough to reply, "Freedom."

The ride to Dire's was quiet, with Mr. Hardwick at the wheel and Eliza sitting between Zilpha and Filemon. Sometime earlier, the snow had stopped. Speckles of white dotted the dead grass beside the gravel road, promising deeper winter in the weeks to come. They took turn after turn, heading farther from the Parletts' and closer to Dire's, and all the while, Eliza's thoughts circled back to Winnie who flew somewhere overhead.

"The cost and reward of Dire's bargains are the same," Mr. Hardwick said, his voice nearly too hushed to hear. "They aren't separate. There's no getting and losing. The getting and losing are wrapped up in one. Remember when you speak to Dire, Eliza: the words we say are not always the words we mean. Know this, and go at things sideways with Dire." He parked the motorcar in front of Dire's house, then got out, seeing as how Eliza couldn't exit through the passenger side door without Zilpha tumbling to the ground. Eliza reached into the glove compartment and pulled out the deck of cards Zilpha carried there. She shuffled through, searching for one card in particular.

Filemon touched her shoulder, a small dusting of a moment that drifted away nearly as quickly as it happened. "Sometimes, I wonder if Dire is tired. Bri told me once that he and his friends would dare each other to come down here in the middle of the night. Dire would always be awake, walking back and forth through the house."

Eliza said, "He told me once that he never sleeps, that the only dreams he dreams belong to other people, never himself. Maybe if he had a good night's sleep, he'd be better at his magic."

"Or maybe if he slept, he'd stop hearing people's dreams altogether."

"Maybe his magic would stop." Eliza rubbed the card in her

hand. "Maybe that's what Dire had wanted when he'd tried to take Pa's sleeping draught from the Fen Jester."

Filemon followed his dad out of the car so Eliza could climb out.

"It's worth a try," Mr. Hardwick said after both he and Filemon slid back in. He leaned out the window then, a small bottle of Pa's tonic in his hands.

Eliza took it and cradled it in her palms. "How…"

"Zilpha. I felt it bumping against my heels, while I drove."

Eliza clenched the bottle's neck in one fist and then stuffed it into one of her pockets. She nodded. She would have to do this—she *could* do this. "I'm going to make a bargain, and I think the people in town would like to know, Mrs. Chess, especially. If you tell her what's going on, she'll make sure everyone else on Fen knows. Maybe it's time everyone bargains for the same thing. We shouldn't have to trade our lives for freedom, like Bri did."

Filemon glanced at his dad, and back at her. "Be safe," he said, giving her a kind, lopsided grin.

Eliza walked alone toward Dire's front door. It stood open. Of course he had known she would come, and of course she found him sitting at the kitchen table, shuffling his deck of cards.

Eliza took in the scene. She listed all the things she was willing to give up, to lose, to change for this to work: *everything.*

This was what she had always known—she would lose herself before she lost Winnie.

Dire pulled out a chair, one close to the window and the *whooshing* of the ocean beyond. It pulled at her, pressing hard against her skin and sending tremors through the parts of her that didn't quite feel real.

"A game then?" Dire asked. "An answer to a question, if you win?"

"This time, I don't care about answers to questions." She sat in the chair Dire offered. She shuffled the cards just as Dire had. She doubted it mattered—the deck was not a normal deck, though that didn't quite matter either. When clear words mattered the most, they seemed to leave her. She tried, *tried* to explain to Dire. "My sister is my best friend. She is part of me."

"I had a best friend once." Dire didn't look at her; nonetheless, she saw sorrow lining the small wrinkles beside his eyes. "I've had plenty of other friends too."

"Magical wolves aren't friends. They're servants." She laid out the cards as required for Kings and Queens, dealing enough for both Dire and her to play. She fanned out her hand, finding the Queens of Hearts and Clubs there. She lay them down. "I want to make a bargain."

"I thought you never dreamed, Eliza. You have to be able to dream to be able to bargain."

"I *always* dream," she said through gritted teeth. Because of her mother's leaving, she had believed the price for dreaming was too high, when truly, the price of never dreaming was that she'd stopped knowing how to live. *That* is what had brought her to this point. "I dream every night. I just know better than to *admit* it."

Dire's clouded eye focused on her.

"Why do you do this?" Eliza asked. "Why do you put Fenians in this position? We *circle* around you like you're gravity, and you play games with us."

He drew a card and lay it down—the King of Diamonds—without looking at it. "I am not the sun, Eliza. I am the moon. I am not gravity. *You* are. You have all the power here, just as everyone on Cape Fen does. You have the power to strike a bargain; I merely have the magic to make it happen."

"You're not the moon."

"I might as well be."

"You're *not*." Eliza could believe in shape-shifting magic, in Dire taking animal abilities and giving them to humans, but for some reason, it was another thing entirely to believe that the moon could be a man. She reordered her cards, drawing two and laying down others. She found the Queen of Diamonds and placed it beside the others. She needed one more to win. The Queen of Spades.

Dire said, "What does it matter if I am the moon or not? I

have the moon's magic. It's dreaming magic. I make your dreams come true…although, rarely does anyone ever seem happy with the results."

"Why would they be happy, when they end up with animal ears and poison skin and…" Eliza stopped, knowing that most of the bargains people had—like Mr. Hardwick and Mrs. Gorham's—were probably invisible, some animal instinct Dire had given to them, instead of a physical trait.

"I do my best."

"Your best isn't good enough."

Dire met her gaze, the clouds inside his eye swirling in the pattern of nighttime fog lit by a lighthouse. "I never wanted this. My grandmother and mother loved the magic, but I never wanted it."

"I never wanted it either," Eliza said.

"And yet here we both are, playing a terrible game of magic our mothers handed down to us."

"You could have made different choices. You could have done better." Eliza drew another card, but then crumpled all of the ones she held in her fists. "You're *lonely*. All this time, my ma was here with you. Did her pretend friendship make you happy?"

Dire flinched. The small movement was enough to tell Eliza that she'd hurt him.

"Why a wolf at all? The first wolf died! Why not let it end?"

"End? There's no end in this. Not for me. *I am not the sun!*" He folded his cards into his hands, the edges pressing hard into his skin. Desperation filled his voice. "You have a choice to bargain or not. I do not have a choice in this. I never have."

Dire felt bad for himself. Eliza knew it the same way she knew when Winnie felt bad for herself because she had to eat oatmeal for the twentieth breakfast in a row. So perhaps this was it: Dire hated the magic he'd inherited. His loathing had meant he never learned how to understand his powers, which meant he had little control over it.

The words we say are not always the words we mean. Go at things sideways with Dire, Mr. Hardwick had said, and so Eliza took his advice. She wasted no more time. She leaned forward in her chair, disguising her motions as she reached into a skirt pocket. She lay out her cards, the extra Queen of Spades she'd stolen from Zilpha's deck among them.

"I win," she said.

"You cheated." Surprise tinged Dire's voice.

"*I never set any rules,*" said Eliza. She would cheat until the end of time if it meant saving her sister. Winnie might choose to be the owl today, but she might not choose it tomorrow. Eliza would bargain for Winnie now, tomorrow, and always.

"What is it that you would like with your winnings, then? The truth of the person behind the Wolf? The *what, where, why* of your sister?"

"No." She cut her hand through the air, the Queen of Spades poised between her thumb and pointer finger as if it were a knife. She knew better than to fall for Dire's tricks. She knew now to go at him sideways. While the truth about Winnie was what she needed most, she buried this dream deep and asked for the story that began it all. The story Pa had never had the courage to ask. "Tell me the origin story of the bargain my mother made."

"I can't tell you about your mother's bargain."

"Then tell me about *mine*. You can do that, can't you? Tell me about *me*."

Dire's moon-cloud eye glimmered. He leaned close. And the tale spooled free.

～

Tynne Serling dreamed of children. Two of them. Two little girls. But she and Waylon couldn't have babies, and so she found herself standing at Baron Dire's doorstep. Her husband didn't want her to do this; in fact, he didn't know she was here. She hated the trickery, but she felt worse for the hurt it would do to Zilpha—among their Parlett family, she was Zilpha's only lifeline. She prayed her sister would forgive her.

At the start of winter, she knocked on Dire's door, and somehow, though she said nothing when he opened it, he already knew the contents of her dream.

"You want daughters, but my magic can't place a child made of you and Waylon inside your body," Dire said. "What then would you make your children from?"

Pretending confusion, Tynne thought for a moment, even though she'd already known he would ask this. She'd studied stories of the Dire's magic long enough, and she'd had her answer planned for months—years, really. She said, "I will think on it and bring it to you."

"What are you offering in return?"

"Friendship," Tynne said. While Dire thought he was giving her two children, what he was really gifting the world was two girls who would love one another as deeply as sisters could. But she didn't dream of this part. Dire's magic twisted dreams, and so she dreamed only of two babies to fill her home and her heart. She didn't dream of girls who would be best friends, who would protect one another from whatever life tossed their way. She hoped the dream she allowed him to see would become something beautiful, because of the secret dream hidden beneath it.

Dire's moon-clouded eye fixated on her, and in it, Tynne saw the loneliness of the space between the stars in the night sky. "You bargain for daughters, and you offer me your friendship in return?"

She knew Dire didn't understand friendship that was truly, freely given, that existed selflessly, like the friendship that lived between Tynne and Zilpha. Tynne knew too that though Zilpha loved Dire, it wasn't enough. Because of his magic and his life, something inside Dire was confused, and because of it, friendship was a thing he would barter for.

Knowing this, she said, "But not until I've had a chance to raise my girls."

"Eight years. You can have eight years to raise them."

"And after that, I will be your Wolf for two. One year for each girl."

"Six years. Three for each."

Tynne worried at her lower lip. She would split the time down the middle. She didn't like the idea of leaving her daughters for so long, but Waylon would do a good job of caring for them; he would have to. "Two for each girl. Four years total. Promise—" She caught herself. Dire's promises were worthless— Zilpha had told her that much. "Make it part of the bargain."

"Done."

Tynne bent to where she'd stowed a small sack, no longer pretending. "Then I would make my first child from the ocean, from *this*—" She opened the large canvas bag, revealing the gasping form of a baby sea-pup she'd found abandoned. A moment passed, and suddenly a human baby—black haired and black eyed with fat crocodile tears dripping down her cheeks—laid on the stoop instead of the pup.

But even as Tynne crooked her arms to scoop her baby girl, *Eliza*, against her chest and wrap her into the folds of her dress, Eliza's sticky skin slithered beneath her hands, trying to transform back into a seal.

"They must stay human!" Tynne cried out, her mind scampering for purchase against this unanticipated twist. "The bargain said they stay human!"

"I'm sorry, but the bargain said nothing about them staying in the human form you chose for them."

"*Dire!*"

"Four years of your friendship is worth two transformations, but whether your children stay human or return to their original form will be their choice."

Desperation wrenched a sob from Tynne's throat.

"*But…*" Dire said.

Hope brightened in her.

"You have eight years with them, so your daughters will have eight years as well. The bargain won't touch them until your service begins."

"Nor will it touch them after it ends. If they stay human through the years I spend with you, then they stay human for good."

Dire closed his eyes. He seemed tired, and for this she almost felt bad. *Almost.*

He said, "This is the bargain then: your children will stay human, *purely* human, but they will have the choice during your years as Wolf. If they choose to stay human through your four years, they will stay human for good. After that, the magic won't be able to alter them."

"Four years is a long time." She looked up, agreement making her tighten her hold on Eliza. "Four years, and they will be free from magic until they are *both* eight."

"Done," Dire said, and Tynne felt the bands of the bargain tighten around her. "And what will your second child be made from?" Dire asked.

"I was not prepared for you to agree to two daughters. I will bring to you what the second should be made from soon."

Dire narrowed his eyes. He seemed to know what Tynne was thinking, the trick she hoped to play, but she no longer cared if he knew, the bargain was already set in place. She couldn't undo what had already been done.

~

Dire's rueful smile cut Eliza deep. He said, "It was only as the years passed, and I didn't see Tynne again, that I realized my mistake."

Eliza had listened to Dire's fast-spoken tale, feeling the

press of her swollen and heated skin, craving the ocean more than she craved the earth beneath her feet, and smelling the scents of the Wolf from where it once walked through the parlor. It made sense now, didn't it? She was made from the skin and bones of a seal.

"Did you catch it? Your ma said, 'Four years, and they will be free from magic until they are both eight.' Unknowingly, I agreed to a bargain where magic couldn't touch either of you until you *both* were past your eighth birthday. Your mother would turn Wolf when her *eldest* child turned eight, and from there would serve for four years—until you turned twelve. Tynne thought that if she waited until you were at least five for Winnie to be created, her service would end before *both* of you turned eight. My magic would never be able to tempt you away from being human."

"But Winnie and I are three years, eleven months, and three weeks apart." Eliza well knew the distance between her and Win. "We needed to be at least four years apart for Ma's plan to work."

"I realized that if I let any more time pass, the second child would be born too late. Your mother thought she fooled me, but if I would've allowed it to happen, the magic of the bargain would've fallen apart altogether. No one understands how tricky magic can be. I had to do something. So one week before your fourth birthday, I appeared on the Jester's doorstep with a small owlet in my hands. I told your mother that she'd run out of time and that I'd made the choice for her."

"Your magic only had one week to try and make us transform—between Winnie's eighth birthday and my twelfth, when Ma's bargain ends."

"Only one week to convince you to shift into your animal forms."

"This was why the Wolf came," Eliza whispered. She knew so much now: why the Wolf had appeared right after Winnie's birthday, why the Wolf had never approached before this year, why this all happened *now* instead of in years past. Dire's magic could only work after Winnie's birthday, when they were both over the age of eight.

"Ma-the-Wolf came," Eliza said, wonder making her words shine bright and warm in her mouth, "to call her own bargain to a close."

TWENTY-TWO

*Tynne Serling dreamed. She shaped her daughters,
building miniature galaxies inside their hearts. Love
streamed to their fragile toenails, to the ridges of their
fingerprints, to the knobs of their knees, to the thin
muscles between their ribs, to the gentle lining inside
their skulls, and at last, to the unbreakable bond
between them. She dreamed of this and made it so.*

E liza had an origin story. Not one that went: once upon a
time, two people fell in love; they had a baby and named
her Eliza.

Rather, it's the one that went: once upon a time, Eliza discovered her lungs held air better underwater than they did on land.

Ma used to say, *Eliza, you'd hold your breath for an eternity if you thought it would fix everything. You're just stubborn enough to convince your lungs they can pack triple the oxygen, to teach your body to shunt blood from your limbs to your heart and brain, and to fool your muscles into bearing the strain of a deep-water dive.*

What Eliza never knew, though, was if this was just another story Ma told to pretty up the unbearable world. She knew now that it hadn't been. It had never been *just* a story. It had been the truth.

Then, because now was as good of a time as ever, and because the courage Pa lacked filled her to the brim, she pulled from her pocket the tiny bottle of sleeping draught Mr. Hardwick had handed her.

"I brought you a gift," she said.

Surprise lifted Dire's brows and drew Eliza's focus to his clouded eye, wondering if he would see through the trick she played.

"I knew you wanted to try it." She placed the bottle on the table and scooted it toward Dire. "You said you never sleep. Maybe tonight would be a good night to try. You have to drink it all for it to work."

Dire didn't glance away from her. He took hold of the bottle, one finger resting on the cap.

"Colby said that you think Zilpha betrayed you," Eliza said. "But I don't think she did. I think she misses you."

Dire looked up from the bottle. "I miss her as well, but it's difficult to be friends once they've betrayed you."

"You were one the one who made her sister disappear."

"Tynne came to *me*, and then Zilpha came to *me* to bargain. They chose to use me for my magic."

"It's not betrayal when someone asks for help. I've learned how to ask Filemon for help, and all it means is that I trust him," Eliza said.

She looked at each of her graying, aching fingers. Her ma had lived with dreams at her fingertips, weaving strands of starlight to protect against the winter. But she'd bargained and disappeared, and her leaving had exposed Eliza to the cold. To stay safe, Eliza had stopped dreaming. Stopped doing anything at all except surviving day to day. And a life without dreaming wasn't much of a life at all.

That's the life Dire had. He stole dreams from others and used them to make magic, but he never slept and never dreamed his own dreams. She refused to be like him a moment longer.

Eliza pushed up from her chair. She knew what to offer to save Winnie. Her mother had shown her what to do. "Ma's wolf-bargain will end on my birthday. You'll need another wolf after that. So, I will give you friendship."

Her arms hovered at her sides. The two parts of her warred, feeling as though fire lit her from within. The first part—the one she'd built in the years since Ma left, who quieted her dreams, and who bent to fear and denied the world she loved—was nothing but a disguise. It was a coat she'd tugged on four years ago for comfort and then had forgotten to ever take off.

Eliza relaxed, opened her hands, and the two tangled parts of her slipped apart.

"I will be your friend," she told Dire. Relief poured through her muscles. She felt the calm of swimming in the depths of the ocean. "I want to bargain *for* Winnie. I will be your friend. I will turn into an animal, but if I do this, then Winnie keeps her choice. She keeps *both* her forms, forever. She doesn't have to choose."

"Done," Dire said without looking at her. He pried loose the wax that held Pa's sleeping draught closed.

The suddenness of his acceptance startled her. She'd thought he would barter longer like he had in the story with her ma. The bargain tightened around her.

"Winnie doesn't have to choose," Eliza repeated to herself.

Dire's mouth creased at the edges, not quite a smile and not quite a frown. It was something in between that reminded

Eliza of long, sleepless nights. He said, "That was the bargain we agreed to," before taking the smallest sip of Pa's tonic.

Wildness rushed through her. Just like her mother, she'd bargained, but not for herself. *Never* for herself, and that's where Dire had just gone wrong. "I have all the power here. Not you."

He looked up from the bottle, caught in the middle of setting it back on the table.

Eliza crossed to the window, undid the latch, and breathed in a rush of salty ocean air. It smelled of days on the beach with Ma, paddling with the tide. "You might be the moon, but I am the earth. You might be the magic, but I am the dream. You might be the bargainer, but I decide the cost and the reward, and my friendship is *both*. I would transform for Winnie, but I was never human to begin with! I never said what animal I would become, and I will not turn into a wolf for you, because *I am not a wolf*; I am a seal. My mother made sure of it, and my mother's bargain comes before yours!"

And with that, she followed after Winnie's lead and she *chose*. She jumped. Air whooshed past her ears. She screamed and squeezed her eyes shut as the world rushed by, as wind snatched at her skin, as her stomach flew into her throat. The fall was too great, and she hit the water too hard. The impact stunned her, vision collapsing inward, fuzzing to black as she plunged beneath the waves. Strong water grabbed her, wrenching her down. This was not the sweet, curling water of Fen Bay, but the harsh, uncontrolled waves beside the cliffs.

She sank beneath the ocean, pulled down by her heavy boots. She kicked them off and scrambled for the surface, but under the waves, there was no sense of up.

One, two, three. She fought the water.

Four, five, six. Her fingers slid through the slick.

Seven, eight, nine. She opened her eyes. Pure black surrounded her like the black behind eyelids in the middle of the night. The black of witching-hour dreams. The black of moonless nights when she woke from nightmares and told stories to stop herself from falling back into sleep.

Fifty-nine, sixty, sixty-one. She stopped struggling against the water and the sense that she didn't belong here. Because she did.

She did.

TWENTY-THREE

—

Eliza dreamed. Water flowed beneath her body and passed over her flippers. Strong muscles propelled her forward, pushing her through the ocean. She swam.

One hundred and three, one hundred and four, one hundred and five. Eliza's bones shifted and slid. Her body flowed and thickened, making room for the inches of blubber that grew between her skin and intestines.

One hundred and ninety-eight, one hundred and ninety-nine, two hundred. Her legs melded together. She swelled, becoming light and smooth in the water.

Two hundred and eighty-one, two hundred and eighty-two, two hundred and eighty-three. Whiskers poked free of her face. A sense of movement zipped into her body, telling her what fish swam around her.

Three hundred and twelve, three hundred and thirteen, three hundred and fourteen. Water pressed against Eliza's thick skin as she swam in the depths. Her eyes widened to catch light bent against streams of liquid. Sharp clicks of sound reached her through the deep.

Six hundred and twenty, six hundred and twenty-one, six hundred and twenty-two. Once upon a time, Eliza dreamed of this. Every night, she had dreamed of the ocean. For her sister, she would live like this. For her sister, she would do anything.

Seven hundred and twelve, seven hundred and thirteen, seven hundred and fourteen. She found the ocean's surface.

She breathed.

TWENTY-FOUR

*Kendare Lovell used to dream. He'd dreamed of
breathing, of being able to inhale, exhale without
tension straining his lungs, of drawing in air even
through the most difficult, impossible moments.
And in the end, Dire had made this dream come
true. Kendare's body breathed water, however
difficult and impossible it was to believe. Sucking
liquid through gills, he'd dragged from it precious
oxygen to fill his blood. But then Kendare had
wanted the dream to disappear, and he'd stayed
on land too long. He didn't dream anymore.*

I t was like this: Dire's bargains sometimes required double the
cost. One year of Mr. Chess's life for Mrs. Chess to find peace.

Both Miss Alayna *and* her baby for Bri's freedom. Two years of friendship-service for each of Tynne Serling's daughters. For Winnie to keep her choice, Eliza needed to leave behind her human form. When you bargained away your option to choose, giving it to your sister, you lived with the consequences.

This then was Eliza's consequence: she would be a seal forever.

And here was what her heart had always dreamed: that the world would stay safe enough for Winnie to live. Winnie *was* a dream. She was how Eliza remembered Ma—a dream in a world that twisted and magicked dreams into terrible shapes. Eliza wouldn't ask Winnie to change who she was, but she would certainly try to change the world into a safe enough place so Winnie could live with all her dreams unbroken. She wouldn't let Win's heart be ruined.

This was Eliza's consequence too: she didn't have a sister in the ocean.

Cards floated at the water's surface. She nudged one with her nose—a Queen of Spades. Either the queen she used to cheat with Dire or the queen he used to cheat in their first game.

She captured the card between her teeth and dreamed now. She dreamed with her eyes open. She dreamed with honest thoughts dancing through her mind. She dreamed in the way she'd never allowed herself to before—at least not since Ma left.

And as she did, as she watched and dreamed, the card changed. A King of Spades glistened on the dark water of the ocean.

She dreamed into the night sky. Of human fingers and human bones and a human heart to power the body. She dreamed of the form Ma had gifted her.

In her bargain with Dire, she hadn't said she would give up being human forever; she'd only said she would turn into an animal. Now, she refused to let fear overtake her. This dream, of being human and animal and everything she needed to survive, she would make a reality. She would do this; she *had* to attempt to turn back human. The old her wouldn't have; the old her would never have known to try.

TWENTY-FIVE

—

Tynne Serling dreamed. She waded belly-
high in water that glittered with moonlight.
The night smelled of footprints left behind
by her daughters. "I'm coming," she sang to
the sky. It was nearly time to go home.

One, two three. Eliza swam the outline of Cape Fen. The
expanse of the ocean spooled out, unending and terrifying, and she wanted the place she'd swum as a child. She entered
Fen Bay, heading toward the beach.

Two hundred and thirty, two hundred and thirty-one, two

hundred and thirty-two. If she had a chance at transforming back human, this was where it would happen.

Five hundred and forty-two, five hundred and forty-three, five hundred and forty-four. She washed ashore, flopping onto her belly, rocks pressing against her body. She knew the scent of this place, and it smelled like home.

She flopped and strained across the rocks, the motion tiring her muscles. Land was not where this body was meant to exist.

Transform! Become human.

But her body didn't change. She stopped moving, gasping at the effort.

Please.

She had hoped that by outsmarting Dire and breaking the bargain with him before it'd even begun, it would mean that like Winnie, she could keep both her forms. She could be human again, and she wouldn't be stuck. But as she lay on the beach with her flippers brushing the rocks, she didn't think that was the case. When at last she could take the feel of the open air against her skin no longer, she gave a desperate cry and made her way back to the water that would be her home forever.

She submerged, the great, salty ocean closing over her.

And just as she was about to push into the depths of the bay with her dream drifting away, her body shifted and changed. Flimsy legs and arms churned at the waves. Thin skin stung with brine and freezing water. Toes caught against the sand and dug in. Waves pressed against her mouth and she told herself to *wait, don't breathe, not yet.* She clawed her way toward the beach and lay face down on the rocks, shudders wracking her muscles. Gasping, cold air entered her lungs.

Ten fingers. Ten toes. Human bones. A human heart. Wet hair streaming around her face. Temperatures her human body couldn't survive.

A white and gray mottled owl landed beside her. Eliza choked on the sob that clawed its way out of her mouth.

"Winnie? But I—but I…bargained. Choice. B-b-barg…"

The owl screeched. The sound pierced Eliza's fragile, water-logged ears.

Warmth tingled through her core and into her muscles. *Not good,* said Eliza's mind. *You are cold; you should feel cold. You are dying if you feel warm.*

The owl disappeared from view. Eliza tried to climb after it, but her strained body fell beneath her exhaustion. Somewhere behind her, the woods crashed. *No.* Something crashed *through* the woods. She tried to look, but her neck stiffened in place.

Momma? she thought, but it wasn't her mother who had come to save her, it was Zilpha, and it was owl Winnie and it was Filemon and Filemon's dad. And Zilpha was covering Eliza over with a jacket and screaming for help and snatching her up into her arms like Eliza was nothing but a wrinkled blanket.

Zilpha carried her through the woods and then they were on Old Queen Mae and they were in the warmth of the Hardwicks' home with Filemon tucking more blankets around her body and Miss Alayna pressing a hot water bottle against her chest. All of this happened somewhere outside of Eliza, because inside she was nothing but tingling warmth, memories of the water, and a last dreadful hope that owl-Winnie would be human-Winnie when she woke.

TWENTY-SIX

—

*Eliza won a game of cards. She folded the
Queen of Spades into a paper ship. Lit its hull
with blue fire. Sailed the ship into the open
space of night, with first mate, navigator, cook,
carpenter, doctor—her family—on board.*

I know it's hard, but you could at least *try*." Eliza stomped
both feet in a gushy pile of snow, angry with her sister in a
way she had never been before. The absence of worry that the
Wolf would kill Winnie had left space for annoyance she both
liked and didn't like at the same time. The end to their mother's

bargain might not have come yet, but there was no longer any bargain over Winnie's head. What happened to Winnie was forever Winnie's choice. *Eliza had won.*

Winnie perched on a tree limb, preening her feathers and ignoring her completely.

Eliza stomped again. "I bargained so that you could *choose*! Oh, don't look at me like that. You're choosing; I get it."

Filemon scrunched a pile of snow between his hands, forming it into a ball. "She's definitely not going turn human with you guilting her like that. She's just like you. Stubborn."

"My birthday celebration's tonight though, and so help her if she chooses to spend it as an owl!"

"She's not going to spend your birthday as an owl. You could try and trust her." Filemon took aim with the snowball.

"If you throw that at me, I am going to tackle you and shove your face into the closest snow drift. You just watch."

Filemon eyed her and launched the ball at Winnie instead, who fluttered off her roost and alighted on the Chesses' roof with ease.

Eliza rolled up her collar and tucked her mittened hands inside her sleeves. It had been two days since nearly dying of the cold and wet and two days since she'd been a seal. She didn't know if she would ever transform back. The thought of getting stuck in animal form was too much for her to bear.

"I won," Eliza said, more to herself than to Filemon. The wonder of it still struck her.

"We all won." Filemon stuck out his elbow, and Eliza threaded her arm through his.

Two nights past, Mr. Hardwick had found Dire asleep at his kitchen table, the bottle of sleeping draught empty. Dire had slept for two days, and while he slept dreamless, his connection with his magic had been severed, and Cape Fen's imprisonment had ended. If Dire wanted it back, he'd have to start from scratch, recreating the first bargain his grandmother had made with Fen when she'd first arrived. Eliza though, hoped Dire wouldn't try. She thought he might've known what would happen when he drank the sleeping draught, and that he'd been seeking escape just as much as the Fenians had. Maybe he'd wanted it to end this way.

Eliza found she couldn't be angry with Dire as she'd once been. She'd believed it his fault that her mother had disappeared, but now she knew it was a much more complicated deal than that.

This was exactly why Eliza had sent Winnie over to Dire's house that morning with a birthday invitation tied to her leg. Winnie had given no indication as to Dire's response.

Eliza led the way down the path through the woods. Chickadees and titmice flittered through the branches, sending out trilling calls that warmed the shadows. She lifted her face to them, reveling in the giddiness that swept through her, free of the exhaustion that once weighed down her limbs.

"I dreamed last night," she said.

"What of?" Filemon asked, as if this change in conversation was nothing interesting and as if he didn't know what it might have once cost her to speak of dreaming aloud—and indeed, Filemon didn't know, which was precisely why she told him her dream.

"Flying. I dreamed of flying, except I was flying away from an awful storm, one of the black-eyed ones where rain comes down sideways and wind tears up roofs."

"That sounds bad."

"It wasn't really." She watched Winnie soar above them. "I liked flying, and the rain was nice."

"Sideways rain was nice? Remind me of that the next time a hurricane hits the coast."

Together, they arrived at school where the world continued on as if nothing changed, when in fact everything had, because—

"Dad said we're going to vacation on the mainland. I've never been to the mainland before," said one of the girls, as if *any* of them had vacationed on the mainland before.

The original bargain had been broken, which meant that now, they were free to go. Permanently, or just for vacation. After all, Cape Fen was beautiful. Who would ever want to leave?

"Bri's coming home from university," Filemon said as he passed by Miss Alayna's small desk at the front of the class.

"I know," Miss Alayna said, uncertainty warring over her features. "He said he's planning on coming back for two weeks over his winter holiday break. Now have a seat. Today, we study the story of a man who caught the devil in a sack."

"Please," Colby Parlett said from where she lounged in her seat, feet kicked up to brace the bottom of her boots against the backside of her brother's chair. "You don't catch the devil in a sack. Right, Eliza?"

Eliza grinned at her cousin, hearing the truth of the story Colby told. "Of course not. You catch him in a bargain."

~

Pa had the Jester packed with people by the time Eliza made it home from school. She knew that the rest of Cape Fen wasn't celebrating her birthday—really, on Fen, birthdays had never been a thing to throw big parties over—but the day was a good excuse for adults to gather and gossip over what had happened.

Pa gave Eliza a squashed hug when she arrived and placed something in her palms. He winked once but walked away before she peered down at it. When she unfolded her fingers, she found a small wooden carving of a harbor seal settled warm against her skin. She cupped it tight, ran her thumbs over its smooth back, and examined the long whiskers carved into its face.

"I heard there was a party."

Everyone froze, Dire included. He braced himself in the doorway of the Jester, tense shoulders raised toward his ears. The set of his body, wrapped tight in a black wool coat that hung to his knees, looked like the pause of breath after a question asked.

Nearly too quiet to hear, as if the Jester were no louder than mornings before anyone woke, he said, "I was invited this time, if it helps."

"It's true. I sent him an invitation." Eliza tucked the seal into the pocket of her coat. She crossed the room. The crowd parted for her just as easily as it parted for Dire. They met in the middle.

He fished in his coat for a moment, and then drew out a pack of cards. "I didn't know if gifts were acceptable, but I thought you might like these."

Eliza squinted up at him. "Are there two Queens of Spades?"

"Not anymore."

She beamed. "Then I'd like to play a game later, if you'd like."

"I would. I would like that very much." Dire moved through the crowd, meeting up with Zilpha near the bar, and Eliza hoped that he'd be able to figure out how to talk to people without the constraints of the bargains around him.

"Sometimes I wonder where he goes during the summer," Colby said from behind her.

"Huh?"

"He winters here and leaves come summer, which means he goes somewhere *else* during summer."

Eliza's fingers pat-patted the seal in her pocket. She'd never thought about this, and she found that she didn't want to think on it now, either. Or really, ever.

"I heard there was a party."

This time, it wasn't the crowd that froze, it was only Eliza, for it seemed she was the only one who heard the softly spoken voice of the person who stood in the Jester's doorway.

Silent tears coursed down Eliza's cheeks. Not a single noise tripped from her throat as she was pulled toward the door. As she fell into gravity. As she was tumbled down, broken apart, and pieced together within the span of one breath. As a bridge traversed the rifts inside her, because her mother—her glorious, human-shaped mother—raised her arms to catch Eliza. She pressed her face to her mother's chest and wet her shirt with the sobs that pulled from the very center of her heart.

And then it was Pa and owl-Winnie who were there as well, tangling themselves into the warmth and safety of their family.

That night, the four of them fell asleep on cots at the back of the Jester. Ma. Pa. Eliza. Winnie. It was as if Eliza saw eight though instead of four—who they had been and who they were now—each of them carrying broken pieces that would take time to heal. But at least they were together. At least they had the chance to mend.

Winnie had settled down for night in her owl form. Eliza had been convinced Winnie didn't know how to change back human. Every time she asked, Winnie turned away, stubborn as ever.

But Winnie wasn't an owl now; she'd shifted sometime after falling asleep. She was a girl with hair so light the tips rose in the heat given off by the potbelly stove. Her soft inhalations filled the room to the brim.

Eliza closed her eyes.

And she dreamed.

ACKNOWLEDGMENTS

As many people have said before me, writing a book is not a solo endeavor. There are so many people to thank:

Natalie Lakosil, for pulling me out of the slush and for being willing to stick with me. Your enthusiasm and support and complete kindness has been a pure gift. I will *never* forget your surprise phone call and hearing of the offer. That moment will live inside me forever.

Annie Berger, for loving my wolf book and having a vision that shined up the rough parts. You knew exactly what to say to help me transform this manuscript. Working with you has been a dream. The entire team from Sourcebooks has been just magnificent. I could never have asked for a more wondrous experience for my debut. Thank you to everyone who's played a role in bringing my book to life: Cassie Gutman, Lynne Hartzer, Heather Moore, Mallory Hyde, Ashlyn Keil, Nicole Hower, Jana Heidersdorf, Travis Hasenour, Danielle McNaughton, Dominique Raccah, Todd Stocke, Margaret Coffee, Heidi Weiland, and Valerie Pierce.

Lacee Little, your friendship has sustained me in ways I cannot express. You have propped me up countless times and have been a constant, consistent source of strength and wisdom. My gratitude for your unfailing generosity, your honesty in my work, and your undying love for Dianna Wynne Jones.

Lauren Spieller, you were the first I called with my news for a reason. You've been with me nearly from the start of this long, long journey and know the ups and downs better than nearly anyone. Thank you for always being willing to tell me what I needed to hear instead of what I wanted to hear. I'll put it in writing: you're always right.

Mary Parton, for being a champion and a transformative friend. Emily Neal, for being the absolute best guide in what books to read. Kurt Hartwig, for writing pirates with me when I was sure I'd never figure out how to write again. Rebecca Petruck, for opening your home and your heart, and for making the most delicious scrambled eggs I've ever had. Mel Stephenson, for insisting I learn how to say thank you when complimented and that I treat myself in healthy ways. Rebecca Enzor, for being logic when I didn't understand what was going wrong in my writing.

David and Cathy Bock, Maria Stout, Jessica Vitalis, Tara Creel, Kara Seal, Mare Hagarty, Alexandra Alessandri, Kate Foster, Laurie Lascos, Bronwyn Clark, and Ron Walters, for reading early drafts. Your enthusiasm and hope for this story gave me clarity and inspiration.

The #PitchWars team, for providing me with an outlet for writing, where I could give back to the community and push my own skills forward in a positive way. Stacy Hackney, Julie Artz, Lacee Little, Bronwyn Clark, and Lorelei Savaryn. You were the best mentees a mentor could ever hope for. Thank you for my owl necklace.

My path to publication was not a straight one. At its core, *The Wolf of Cape Fen* is about a girl learning to accept and be honest about her dreams and understanding that her dreams are what will inevitably save her, despite how difficult they are to admit to. Keeping this in mind, I send a quiet, heartfelt thank-you to the thirteen manuscripts I wrote before *The Wolf of Cape Fen*. They taught me everything I know about writing.

And lastly, but firstly, thank you to my family:

My parents, Marsha and Randy Brandt. Your steadfast faith that I would be published someday always seemed silly to me. How could you possibly know such a thing? But as always, you knew what I did not. Your unwavering belief in me gave me the space to dream brilliantly and the dedication to keep going, even when the road was tough. I could never say thank you enough for that.

My sister, Katie Woodard. I wrote this story as a way to understand and share what it was like growing up with you as my big sister. You always let me be as dreamy and wild as I needed, and because of that, I always felt safe and loved being exactly who I was. You are my Eliza. This book is for you. Thank you.

READ ON FOR
AN EXCERPT OF ANOTHER
MAGICAL NOVEL
FROM JULIANA BRANDT

Coming May 2021

ONE

The valleys in Appalachia were all dressed for an outing.
Red pom-pom frocks and green needle suits draped
over the trees. Strands of ribbon vines hugged their necks. Shoes
of crimson and orange leaves clung to their feet. The valleys and
surrounding mountains were glimmering, and they were dressed
to the nines...but that did not describe the valley in which
Sybaline Shaw lived. The valley in which Sybaline Shaw lived
made all those *other* valleys shed their leaves and tuck themselves
into bed for the winter, ashamed they hadn't shown up to the
autumn party in even finer dress.

Her valley was more than glimmering. It was *magical*.

The warmth of her mountains filled her to the brim as she
sat at her kitchen table and ground corn with her handheld mill.
She stared out the open front door. Smoke crept between the
boughs, a haze that hung along the horizon. Past that, the sun

rose high over the eastern side of the valley, spotlighting the quilted mountains in a blur of light.

The handle of the mill slipped against the calluses on Sybaline's hand. She wiped her palm on her smock and blew on it, drying the sweat on her skin, before grabbing up the spinning handle again. Inside the mill, corn fell through the funnel and into the grinder below. Fresh cornmeal piled into a bowl that she would later cook into flapjacks and cornbread.

Her mother came up the front steps of the porch. Magic warmed in the air and tightened the feeling of the world, as if a lightning storm were about to pass through the valley. Momma'd likely been using the magic to help grow vegetables in the garden: pumpkins, carrots, collard greens. A wide basket filled her arms, piled high with corn. She paused in the threshold, arms tense around the basket.

"Momma?" Sybaline kept turning the mill.

A secret expression crossed Momma's face. Dark hair clung to the perspiration on her neck, sticking to a deep wrinkle in her skin.

"*Momma?*" Sybaline asked.

Momma took a hesitant step into the room, finally saying, "I thought you were sitting in your father's chair."

Sybaline stopped churning, shocked. "I would never."

"I don't know what I was thinking." Momma set the basket

on the table and pressed a kiss with one hand to the air above Poppa's chair. It had sat empty for two years, untouched since the moment he'd stood and walked out the door, answering the summons of the government to go to war.

Sybaline pushed hard on the crank and forced her thoughts away from Poppa and the letter they'd received from him recently. *I'm doing just fine, saw a robin the other day,* he'd written.

"Wooline stopped by while I was gardening. She invited us to a fish fry tonight, and she needs you to go fetch your cousins. She wants them home," Momma said.

"Auntie Wooline always makes me go get them," Sybaline complained, shoving hard against the churn.

"Which means you shouldn't be surprised she's asking you to now. Your cousins listen to you."

"They listen to me because I tell them if they don't, then Auntie Wooline will come for them, and if Auntie Wooline has to drop her work to get them, they'll regret it."

Momma barked out a laugh. "You're their last warning. Better for them that they know it."

Sybaline hated leaving a task unfinished, but still, she unhooked the grinder from where it was clamped to the edge of the table. She put it in its proper place, then stepped into the world outside, with its sun-warmed sky and tender-feathered breeze.

The valley enveloped her, mountains rising in every direction, their leaves stained a hundred different shades of red, orange, yellow, and purple. The pincushion-clouds hovering at their tops were stuck through with wheeling birds.

She headed into the backyard, where endless rows of trees climbed the side of the mountain that towered behind their house. Under their shade, she wiggled her bare toes in the crunchy leaves, finding soft moss hidden beneath. The insides of her body tingled. This was how magic felt, alive and syrupy and warm inside her, almost as if she'd eaten and was full to the brim with good food and happiness.

The magic sparked in her fingertips, and in response, the woods bent toward her. The magic existed in the land, a piece of nature itself. It appeared as a slight dancing of the branches, twigs shivering at her proximity and leaves spinning toward her head. She raised her hands and twirled in the rainbow confetti, laughing loose the tension that had tightened the muscles in her chest while talking with Momma about Poppa.

Momma. Sybaline dropped her hands and the branches snapped back into place, quivering as if a breeze wafted by instead of Sybaline's pull on the magic inside the valley. She was too responsible to play with the magic like this, and if Momma were here, she would remind her of that fact.

Before Poppa had left for war, he'd told Sybaline it was

her job to be exactly as dutiful as Momma needed, which was perfectly dutiful all the time. With both her older brothers moved away, it was up to her to take care of home.

Somber now, Sybaline continued toward the creek that ran through their land and met up with Auntie Wooline's. If they weren't busy with chores, her cousins could usually be found playing games in the stream. The trickling of water came through the forest. She headed toward it and popped out of the path, finding herself on the bank of a small, but swift, creek. Upstream, the water began at a natural spring that was Sybaline's family's water source.

Magic tingled against her bare feet. It told her that someone was using it, and it certainly wasn't her.

It had to be her cousins.

"Where are you?" she asked.

A giggle came from her right, but when Sybaline looked, all she saw was water and stones and woods and leaves and a cluster of vines hanging from a tree limb.

And then, because she knew exactly how to make her cousins do as she wanted, she said, "*Get,*" in her most stern and no-nonsense voice.

Magic warmed the air before her, pushing and pulling at the pieces of nature. Then, water whooshed, making a mini-waterfall that fell in a rush into the creek. Marlys appeared near the right bank, in all her wild-haired glory, and from across the creek, Tevi appeared as well, a small replica of her older sister.

"You're no fun," Marlys said. With magic, she pushed at the last bits of water that clung to her dress, forcing it away from her and into the creek until she was dry.

"You're the opposite of fun," Tevi echoed, trying to do the same as her sister, but of course, her control of magic wasn't as refined, leaving her dress good and damp at the edges.

"I'm plenty of fun, just not when your momma's waiting for you and my momma's waiting for me," Sybaline said, then asked, "Where's Nettle?"

"Dunno," Marlys shrugged.

"Dunno," Tevi said, gaze skittering toward the hanging vine and back to the river, as if she wanted very much to stare at it but knew she shouldn't. It was much the same way she played Old Maid, trying hard not to give away her hand and giving it away all the same.

"You're not very good at camouflage," Sybaline said, looking straight at the vines.

Nettle released the magic that held the vines in a clump around her body. "You wouldn't have known if Tevi hadn't given away my spot."

"I didn't give you away!" Tevi stomped a foot. "I didn't give anyone away."

"You gave *us* away. You're the one who giggled," Marlys pointed out.

Tevi hunched her shoulders and then launched herself across the creek and tackled Marlys into the water.

Nettle joined Sybaline on the bank. She was four weeks younger than Sybaline, and four inches shorter. Her short stature did nothing to hide the energy that vibrated inside her though. She was always the one to propose ideas that would get them into trouble, and Sybaline was left with the task of talking her out of her terrible plans.

Sybaline turned to head down the path. "Y'all are using magic wrong, you know. You shouldn't use magic for—"

"Unnatural reasons. I know, I know, Sybaline. You sound like my momma," Nettle interrupted. "*Don't use magic in ways contrary to the natural world; it'll turn you into a tree as a consequence,* she says."

"I've used magic plenty in all sorts of ways, and I've still never turned into an actual tree," Marlys said as she climbed out of the creek, leaving Tevi behind.

"*Yet,*" said Nettle. "Besides, you wouldn't turn into a tree. You'd turn into a pigweed."

"Would not! I'd be a laurel tree. Something pretty."

"Pretty *and* common." Nettle pointed at a host of laurel bushes only five paces away.

"Common's better than gross, which is what you'd be. You'd be poison oak!"

Nettle swatted at Marlys, who jumped back with a laugh. She grabbed up a stick she'd stuck into the bank and pulled out a stringer from the creek. A line of fish dangled from its end. "We're having a fish fry tonight. I was supposed to run by your house after fishing and invite you. S'pose I'm inviting you now."

"You're too late. Your momma already came by and invited us," Sybaline said.

"I'm going to be in trouble, aren't I?"

"An hour late *and* you hadn't come by our house yet? Probably."

Nettle sighed, though she didn't look all that disappointed. Nettle never stayed unhappy long, no matter what the problem was, not like Sybaline who couldn't ever rid her head of bad news.

Marlys and Tevi barreled down the path, nearly tripping Nettle. They were all mirror images of one another, just different heights, like the steps of stairs. Sybaline looked enough like them that most people knew on sight they were related. They had the same dark eyes, pale skin that burned during the summer, and wispy hair that fell loose from braids by midday.

"Are you coming to the fish fry tonight, Sybaline?" Marlys asked.

"I like fish," Tevi said. "Except...I don't like it when I eat it too fast, because then it makes me puke."

"If you eat anything too fast, you puke," Marlys said. "And you always eat too fast, which means you always puke. You've spent seven years puking."

"Have not!" Tevi said.

"You used to puke up milk when you were a baby."

Tevi growled, but Nettle snapped out a hand and grabbed the back of her dress before she could tackle Marlys again.

The path ended at the cleared field that surrounded Sybaline's house on three sides. They'd come out on the southern edge of Sybaline's house, and from there, Sybaline had a good view of their front porch. This time, it was Sybaline who reached out and grabbed someone. She didn't really pay attention to who, just so long as she stopped the entire group from blundering into the field where anyone would be able to see them.

Momma stood in the doorway, elbows jutting out and body taking up as much space as possible. Auntie Wooline was there. So too was Auntie Pauline, Auntie Jolene, and... Sybaline's jaw dropped. There was Aunt Ethel walking through the eastern edge of the field, looking for all the world like a giant ready to wreak havoc on whoever had disturbed her rest. Aunt Ethel was always the one people wanted on their side if a fight was about to go down.

Sybaline's momma had four sisters, and if *all* the Lark sisters were gathered and it wasn't dinnertime, it meant something big concerning the family had happened.

"Is that a stranger?" asked Marlys.

Sybaline squinted and saw that indeed, among all her aunts, a stubby man wearing a floppy hat stood with his shoulders hunched in a way that made him look as if he were very overwhelmed.

Tevi said, "When I grow up, I want to be a stranger."

"A stranger isn't a *job*, dummy," Marlys said.

"Shh," Sybaline said.

"I could be a stranger if I wanted," Tevi said.

"I said *shush*!" Sybaline bit out fast, her teeth clenched. Tevi looked at her with rounded eyes. "I know that man."

It was a stranger who wasn't a stranger.

A stranger Sybaline had met once before.

A stranger who had come to take them away from the valley.

ABOUT THE AUTHOR

Juliana Brandt is an author and kindergarten teacher with a passion for storytelling that guides her in both of her jobs. She lives in her childhood home of Minnesota, and her writing is heavily influenced by travels around the country and a decade living in the South. When not working, she is usually exploring the great outdoors. You can find her online at julianalbrandt.com.